THE CANDY DAD

Pat Pritchard

ZEBRA BOOKS
KENSINGTON PUBLISHING CORP.

To Meredith and Evan. I may be the parent and you the children, but you have taught me so much about life and love and laughter. Thank you for giving each day of my life meaning.

ZEBRA BOOKS are published by

Kensington Publishing Corp.
850 Third Avenue
New York, NY 10022

Copyright © 1996 by Patricia L. Pritchard

Zebra and the Z logo Reg. U.S. Pat. & TM Off.

First Zebra Printing: June, 1996
10 9 8 7 6 5 4 3 2 1

Printed in the United States of America

One

"I remember, Vickie, I remember," Jesse Daniels assured his favorite, if only, sister-in-law. "I'll bring in the mail, the trash goes out on Tuesday, Lexi sees the orthodontist on Wednesday at three o'clock, and Brittany hates pepperoni pizza." He shifted Vickie's suitcase to his left hand and put his right arm around her shoulders. "Now quit worrying. I'm a responsible adult and I can handle the house and the girls. Besides, I have the three-volume set of instructions you left me."

Vickie stopped walking and looked up to Jesse. "I'm sorry, Jesse. It's just I've never left the girls alone before, and I feel guilty about not taking them with me. I really do know that you'll take good care of everything." Her blue eyes filled with tears.

Jesse led her off to the side of the concourse and out of the stream of people hurrying through Seatac Airport. He pulled her close for a hug. "Vic, now listen. We've gone through all of this. There is nothing wrong with your flying to Hawaii to meet Mark for a fun-filled two weeks in the sun. Lord knows, you haven't seen much of the sun here in Seattle this spring. Just think how happy Mark will be when he finds out his company is surprising him with a vacation in the islands with his best girl. And I get a chance to spoil my nieces to the best of my ability."

After glancing down at his watch, Jesse gently urged Vickie on down the concourse. He automatically adjusted his long-legged stride to more closely match her shorter one. A quick glance at his companion told him that she still was fighting her conscience. He tried again to reassure her fears.

"Come on, Vickie, let me do this. It's my turn to help you and Mark. Think how much you two did for me over the years. Now dry your tears. We have the number where you'll be if we have questions. I don't want you to think about us for the next fourteen days."

"We'll never be able to thank you enough for this, Jesse. I must say that I'm surprised you'd have the time to take over for us. The way your business has been lately, I was afraid that they were keeping you chained to your computer."

"That's what laptops and modems are for, Vickie. Just ask Mark. He gets a lot of his work done on all those airplane rides up and down the coast and over to Honolulu. I'll be able to work out of your house as easily as I can work at the office. Easier, maybe, since I won't have all the constant interruptions I have there."

Vickie made a choking noise. "Yeah, right, Jess. Our house is *always* peaceful and quiet."

Jesse resisted the urge to pat his petite companion on the head. Vickie hated being reminded that both her husband and brother-in-law towered over her even when she wore three-inch heels. Instead, he gave her another quick hug before he left her standing at the gate while he checked with the ticket agent for a boarding pass.

A few minutes later he rejoined Vickie. "They're going to start boarding now. Here's your ticket, your carry-on bag, and some magazines. Relax and enjoy the flight." He grinned wickedly. "I have a feeling you'll be needing all your energy tonight when Mark gets a peek at that sexy new nightie you didn't think I saw you pack!"

His sister-in-law punched him in the arm and they both laughed. Before either of them could say anything else, the ticket agent announced they were boarding the first-class passengers.

"That's you, Vic. Blond, beautiful, and first class all the way. Now scoot before they let on all those plebeians in coach."

He watched as Vickie reached the line forming at the gate. Just before she reached the entrance to the ramp, a look of utter horror crossed her face and she turned back to Jesse. The press of the crowd behind her kept her from running back to him.

"What's wrong, Vic?" Jesse yelled over the noise in the terminal. "Did you forget something?"

"I forgot all about the candy!"

"Candy? Were you taking candy to Mark?" Jesse called back, confused. Judging by the weight of her luggage, he was sure she'd packed everything that wasn't nailed down.

"No, Jesse, it's the Trailblazer candy!" Before she could explain further, the line of passengers carried her beyond the door to the ramp and out of sight.

Jesse shrugged. He always bought candy from the girls like any good uncle would. No reason for concern—he could handle it. Vickie just worried too much.

The traffic on Interstate 5 had been unusually light on the drive home from the airport. In record time, Jesse found himself almost back to Vickie and Mark's house in Mukilteo, a small town overlooking Puget Sound north of Seattle. Though the area was growing rapidly, Jesse liked the fact that it had retained much of its small-town charm. A great place to raise kids—not that he'd ever need a place like that.

Forcing his thoughts back to cheerier subjects, he was glad to have this time away from his office. He was preparing the final drafts for a complex contract negotiation for one of the companies his law firm represented. With any luck, he could fit one and maybe even two hours of solid work in before Brittany and Lexi got home from school. According to one of the many notes Vickie had left him, the girls were due home about four.

He started down the last big hill toward downtown Mukilteo, having trouble holding his beloved car to the 35 mph speed limit. When he reached Goat Trail Road, he turned up the steep lane that led to the house. The towering Douglas firs and alders along the road blocked most of the view of the Sound, but the neighborhood was attractive in a Pacific Northwest way—rhododendrons budding out, candytuft sending cascades of white flowers down rocky inclines, and the first of the plum trees already covered in pink flowers.

When he turned into the cul-de-sac where the Victorian two-story house was located, he noticed a large truck parked in front of the house. Vickie hadn't mentioned expecting any deliveries—must be for someone else in the neighborhood. But as Jesse parked his dark silver BMW in the driveway, the trucker was already out of the cab and heading toward him.

Jesse took off his sunglasses and smiled at the man. "Can I help you?" he asked as he climbed out of his car.

The trucker, already impatient from having to wait, growled back, "Yeah, your candy's here. Where do you want it?"

Jesse shrugged and reached for his wallet. "I'll take it. How much did Vickie put me down for this year?"

The disgruntled driver checked a clipboard in his hand before answering. "Four hundred cases. The usual mixture of chocolate bars, nut clusters, and peanut brittle."

Jesse couldn't believe his ears. "Excuse me, but did you just say four hundred *cases?*"

"Yep, that's right, your group ordered four hundred cases. It's all in the truck." The driver walked away and opened the back of the rig.

Jesse stared after the man, speechless. He had to admit the driver was right—there was at least that much candy on the truck. Somehow he had to keep it there.

"Look, buddy, there's been some sort of mistake. I mean, no one is home who can handle that candy. You'll just have to take it back to wherever you got it." Jesse inwardly cringed when he realized how desperate he sounded. Corporate attorneys shouldn't crack under pressure like this, but if he had to beg to make the candy disappear, fine.

It didn't matter, though, because the driver wasn't listening anyway. He was too busy lifting wooden pallets of candy boxes off his truck with a small forklift. When he had them unloaded, he backed the forklift away from the truck and carried the first load up the driveway.

Jesse gave way in the face of such determination. Considering the trucker was even taller than Jesse's six-two and outweighed him by at least forty pounds, and none of it fat, it was the wisest course of action. Jesse reached the garage door and opened it just seconds before the forklift would have crashed through.

Then Jesse stood back and watched as nineteen other pallets of candy cases were neatly unloaded and stacked in the garage next to the first one. When the driver set down the last case, there was no space left for Jesse's beloved Beamer. From the way Jesse's lungs were struggling, he wondered briefly if the candy took up so much space, there wasn't even room left for air in the garage.

Jesse signed the papers on the trucker's clipboard without reading them. He stood by after the forklift was reloaded onto the trailer and watched the truck rumble back down the hill. In a gesture of denial,

Jesse calmly closed the garage door and locked it. If he didn't look at it, for now he could pretend the damned candy didn't really exist.

He retrieved his briefcase from the trunk of his car, unlocked the front door of the house, walked into the living room, and sank down in Mark's favorite chair and closed his eyes.

Then the quick-witted, articulate attorney felt the chill of the first tendrils of desperation creeping into his heart and mind.

Jesse was numb, overwhelmed, stunned—the list of emotions could go on for hours. He hadn't felt this at a loss since his mother had pulled up stakes fifteen years ago, leaving him in the care of his older brother, Mark.

To be completely honest, he thought ruefully, he'd never been in this exact position before. In fact, he didn't think he knew anyone else who had ever found himself sitting on three cases of chocolate bars, trying to figure out exactly what to do with the other 397 cases of Trailblazer candy stacked neatly in the garage.

Jesse stood up, absently running his hand through his expensively styled reddish-brown hair. Well, no doubt about it, he'd done a number on himself. Short of laying out the money to purchase all the candy himself, he was going to have to figure out a way to get through the next two weeks of baby-sitting his two nieces, dispensing cases of candy to all of their fellow Blazers, and still finish some difficult contract negotiations at work.

Oops, he knew better than to refer to them as Blazers. The first time he'd called them that, his eight-year-old niece, Brittany, had informed him in no uncertain terms that they were no longer called that. She was a member of an Acorn Club, and Lexi, her eleven-year-old sister, was in a Seedling Club.

Well, whatever they were called, he still had the candy. Lots of it.

"Uncle Jess?" Brittany called from the kitchen. "I think this phone call is for you. Can you take it or do you want them to call back?"

No sense in sitting out in the garage staring at nut clusters the rest of the evening. Jesse stood up and took one last look at the cardboard boxes of confectionery sitting where his BMW should be. He shook his head and headed for the phone.

Brittany handed him the phone and then returned to her homework at the kitchen table. As she leaned over to concentrate on the social studies, her shoulder-length blond hair fell forward, obscuring her face from view.

Jesse put his hand over the receiver and whispered to his niece, "Brit, who is it? Did they ask for me by name?"

"No, they wanted to know if the candy mom was home. I figured that was you." She pushed her blue-framed glasses back up her nose and lifted her eyebrows in an expression that said it was all grown-up business and therefore not her concern. Then she went back to her studies.

Bracing himself, Jesse spoke into the phone, "Hello, may I help you?" all the while hoping he couldn't.

Words came tumbling through from the other end of the line. "Isn't Mrs. Daniels there? I was told that she was the candy depot mom for this year. I need to pick up my candy tonight. I mean, I know we're supposed to wait till Thursday night, but we want to start selling at the first possible moment. Can you reach her? I know the candy was delivered today." The high-pitched voice on the other end of the line was breathless but not slowing down.

Jesse decided to interrupt before the nameless lady could get a second breath. "I'm sorry, ma'am, but Vickie was called out of town suddenly. I'm her brother-in-law. I haven't had a chance to find someone else to take the candy. If you'll give me your name and number, I'll have the replacement mom call you as soon as possible." He used his best corporate "this is how it has to be" tone.

It didn't work.

"Well, Mr. Daniels, I just can't wait," the as-yet-nameless woman insisted. "I'll come get my candy now and you write it down and just pass the information on to whoever takes over. Although I don't know who they'd get to fill in at this late date," she added as an afterthought

"No, I can't have you coming over tonight The rules state we don't hand out any candy until Thursday," he said, grasping at the woman's own words, since he had no idea what rules she'd been talking about. "Please call me Wednesday night for an appointment." Before she could say another word, or even her name, he hung up the phone.

Lexi walked into the kitchen wearing hoop earrings that barely cleared her shoulders and bright orange lipstick. The lipstick contrasted vividly with the silver braces that seemed too big for her mouth. "Uncle Jesse, are you cooking dinner tonight? Mom left a year's worth of casseroles in the freezer."

Jesse eyed the phone, afraid that it would ring again, and then looked at the two girls. "Make you a deal, Lexi. You put your mom's earrings back where you found them and wipe off at least the first four layers of lipstick, and I'll treat you to dinner at the restaurant of your choice tonight."

"How did you know the earrings were Mom's?" Lexi grinned as she reached up to unhook the hoops. She had her dad's coloring—the same red-brown hair and brown eyes that Jesse shared. Already, Jesse could almost see the lovely woman she would become in the next few years. Big-brother Mark was in for some hard times when the boys started coming around to see this one.

"I gave them to her for her birthday years ago." Jesse grinned at her. "Now scoot along so we can get out of here before that woman calls back." He gave her a push toward the bathroom door.

Within minutes, they were on their way to a local restaurant that specialized in family-style cooking. His personal favorite was their corned beef and cabbage.

"Boy, Uncle Jesse, that dinner was great! Sure beat any casserole Mom would've left us," Lexi asserted.

Jesse rolled his eyes. "Lexi, a peanut butter and jelly sandwich followed by a hot fudge sundae can't hold a candle to your Mom's lasagna. I'd weigh three hundred pounds in six months if I got to eat Vickie's cooking on a nightly basis."

He shook his head and smiled at his two nieces. "I can't believe both of you ordered peanut butter when you could've had anything you wanted on a three-page menu. Besides, for what those sandwiches cost, I could've bought a case of the stuff at the store. Maybe I should take it out of your allowances."

Both girls just giggled. They knew that they had their uncle wrapped around their little fingers. If they wanted peanut butter sandwiches at outrageous prices, he'd cheerfully pay the check. It was just one of the costs of being an indulgent uncle.

He drove up the hill to the house. "By the way, did you get your homework done before we left, Brittany?"

"No, I've still got some math to do, but it shouldn't take me long," she answered.

Jesse felt bad about panicking over the candy and rushing the kids out of the house. "Sorry, cupcake, I didn't mean to disrupt your studies. It won't happen again. I just wasn't prepared for the candy."

"Oh, that's all right. I'll have time in class tomorrow if I need it."

"How about you, Lex? Do you need any help getting your studies done tonight?"

"Don't have any, Uncle Jesse. I passed the pretest on the spelling words so I don't have to take the regular test tomorrow. I finished the reading assignment on the bus coming home."

As Jesse pulled the car into the driveway, the halogen head-lights illuminated the front porch. A woman was sitting in the old-fashioned swing that hung from the ceiling of the porch. She stood as he stopped the car and set the brake. Panic time. Could it be the phone lady here to demand her rightful share of candy?

The girls climbed out of the car and headed directly for the woman before Jesse thought to ask who she was. From the way they were acting, she was obviously no stranger. He'd forgotten to leave the porch light on, so once he turned off the halogens he couldn't see anything but her profile. He had to admit it was a fine one. He slowly got out of the car and walked toward their unexpected guest.

Rennie Sawyer was lost in thought when she heard the car pull up the driveway. She'd been watching the changing colors of the sunset—fuchsia pinks and burnt oranges that turned into flaming reds as the sun set behind the Olympic Mountains across the Sound.

What was it that Robin had always said about Puget Sound skies? Oh, yes, he believed the sky here had more layers to it than anywhere else he'd ever been. Of course, that was before he stopped watching sunsets and started living off the adrenaline surges of the stock market.

Before her thoughts could follow that depressing memory any further, a BMW had driven into the driveway behind her. Mrs. Billings, another Trailblazer leader, had called Rennie about an hour before, babbling about a man holding her club's candy hostage. According to the voluble woman, he'd point-blank refused to set a time when she could pick it up.

Rennie suspected that Mrs. Billings had tried to get her candy earlier than the rules allowed, but that was an annual event. If she hadn't also insisted that Vickie Daniels had skipped town right when the candy sale was starting, Rennie would have listened sympathetically and then just ignored the whole situation.

Vickie was famous for her deft running of the candy depot, the Trailblazer name for a central location where several clubs in a given neighborhood took delivery of their candy. It took hours of work over a three-week period to hand out the candy and keep track of the money. If Vickie was gone, it could get ugly real quick.

So with some misgivings, Rennie had walked the two blocks to the Daniels house, only to find no one there. Rather than head back home right away, she'd decided the view of the sunset was worth watching. She sat down on the porch swing and hoped the Daniels family would return shortly. She knew Vickie, of course, and Rennie was the leader of the Trailblazer Club for Brittany Daniels and her own daughter, Becky. Rennie had never met Vickie's husband, though, and that appeared to be who was driving up with the girls.

Brittany was the first out of the car. She came running across the yard. "Mrs. Sawyer! Is Becky here, too?"

"No, not tonight, Brittany. She went shopping with her grandmother and she's not back yet." Rennie smiled and nodded at Lexi as the eleven-year-old came up on the porch and unlocked the front door. Both girls disappeared inside. She blinked against the glare of the porch light that Lexi had turned on.

"Were you waiting to see us about something?" a masculine voice spoke from behind her at the bottom of the porch steps.

Rennie tried to tell herself that it was the chill of the spring evening that caused her to shiver, but in truth it was the pleasantly deep resonance of the man's voice. She turned to face him.

"Mr. Daniels? I'm Brittany's Trailblazer leader, Rennie Sawyer." She held out her hand in greeting. It felt lost in the large hand that enveloped it.

"I'm glad to meet you, Rennie," Jesse answered. "And please call me Jesse. Now what can I do for you?"

Rennie quickly squelched the thought that there was a lot he could do for her. The man was tall and moved with an athlete's easy grace.

His smile would attract women like fire drew moths, irresistible despite the imminent danger of being burned by the flames. Even Rennie's usual caution around all men didn't stop her hand from itching to brush an unruly lock of hair back from his forehead.

The strength of her reaction surprised her. Men normally didn't affect her so easily—not to mention that she was talking to a married man, and the parent of one of her daughter's best friends to boot. She forced her wayward thoughts to the business at hand.

"Well, I'm not sure how to start. Is Vickie going to be home this evening? She's the one I really need," Rennie's voice ended on a hopeful note.

Jesse smiled and shook his head. "I'm sorry, but Vickie's gone to Hawaii for the next two weeks. It's just the two girls and me here. Did you need something?"

Rennie was getting alarmed. "Vickie left when the candy was due in? It's not like her to leave without telling someone beforehand."

"Well, the trip came up so suddenly, she probably didn't get a chance to let you know. I thought I'd call the Trailblazer office tomorrow and see if another mother could take over the candy."

His matter-of-fact assumption that it would be easy to find another mother with time to spare annoyed Rennie. "And if another mother isn't available, Mr. Daniels, what then? Are you really going to hold our candy hostage like Mrs. Billings said?"

"Who's Mrs. Billings?" Jesse asked. Then he realized that she had to be the rapid-fire talker who'd called earlier. "She must be the one who phoned before dinner. I was still pretty much in a daze after all that candy showed up. I didn't threaten to hold the stuff prisoner, I just suggested she wait till another mother could be found."

Rennie was beginning to fume. "Mr. Daniels, I realize that most men feel that parenting is a female occupation, but don't you think for this once you could at least try to help Vickie. Unlike me she is *not* a single parent. Since she was called out of town on an emergency, you ought to be able to fill in for her."

Now she wasn't the only one confused and more than a little angry. "Look, lady, if you want to fight with me, fine. But let's do it inside so we don't provide a show for the neighbors."

"By all means, Mr. Daniels," Rennie snapped. "Let's keep up

appearances. We might be too busy to do something to help the girls, but heaven forbid we fight in public."

Jesse wasn't sure how they'd gotten off to such a bad start, but he wished they hadn't. The promising profile he'd noted outlined by his headlights hadn't done Rennie Sawyer justice. She came up to the top of his shoulders, with a good percentage of that height invested in some terrific long legs, framed nicely in snug jeans. Her dark hair was pulled up in a ponytail that bounced with an angry swish as she marched into the house ahead of him.

Though her friendly smile had disappeared, the high cheekbones and large dark gray eyes were still in evidence. He suspected that when she wasn't frowning so hard that her lips would be soft, full, and very inviting—even if she was a most aggravating woman.

Once inside the house, he motioned for her to wait in the living room so they could discuss the candy problem in private. Before joining her, he wanted to make sure the girls didn't need him for anything. They had gone into the kitchen. He could hear the soft murmur of their voices muffled by the closed door that connected the two rooms.

He opened the door and leaned in. Both girls were sitting at the kitchen table looking at Brittany's math book. "You two all right?"

Lexi answered without looking up. "Yeah, we're cool."

"Okay, I'll be in the other room with Ms. Sawyer. If you need anything, yell."

They went back to work without answering, so he shut the door.

"Please be seated, Ms. Sawyer," Jesse offered when he stepped into the living room, gesturing with his hand to indicate that she should take her pick of the comfortable chairs that flanked the brick fireplace. He chose to sit on the light blue floral couch that faced both the chairs and the hearth. Jesse leaned back and stretched his long legs out in comfort.

Rennie, on the other hand, still appeared to be annoyed with him. Instead of sinking back into the inviting comfort of the loose-cushioned chair, she perched on the edge of the seat. She looked as if she was ready to bolt for the door with the slightest provocation.

"Now, before we resume our discussion"—Jesse's lips quirked up in a smile at the euphemism—"can I offer you anything? Coffee, tea, or . . ." He let his voice trail off at the end.

"No, thank you, Mr. Daniels. I'm sure you have nothing I'd be interested in," Rennie almost snarled back.

From past experience, Jesse knew women generally found him attractive, likable even. He'd never had a woman react so adversely to him, especially when he had no idea what was making her so angry.

Jesse shrugged it off. "Well, then, if I can't do anything to make you more comfortable, I guess we can get back to the matter at hand. What do you suggest I do with the candy?"

Rennie bit back her first answer.

Jesse realized what she was thinking and had to laugh. "Why, Ms. Sawyer! And you a club leader, too."

Chagrined, Rennie tried again. "Mr. Daniels . . ."

"Jesse."

"Okay, Jesse. I don't know what to tell you. At this late date, I really don't think you're going to have any luck in foisting the candy off on anyone else. I'm afraid you're just going to have to muddle through the best you can." She gave him a tight smile.

All Jesse could think of was the work waiting for him in his briefcase. No wonder Vickie laughed when he had remarked he was looking forward to some quiet time away from the office.

"The problem being, of course, Ms. Sawyer . . ."

"It's Rennie."

"Rennie, then. I don't have any idea how Brittany and Lexi are supposed to sell that much candy." The very idea was appalling.

Suddenly Rennie realized that Jesse didn't have a clue what was going on.

"That candy is for eight clubs, not just for your girls. Vickie volunteered to be the candy depot, which means that all the candy for those clubs is delivered here. From here, it gets dispensed to the candy mom in each club. The Trailblazer kids get the candy from their own candy mom. You just have to make appointments for each candy mom to pick up her allotment, and then make sure the money is right when the sale is over in three weeks. If I heard you right, Vickie will be back before the final paperwork needs to be done."

She leaned back into the chair and thought for a minute. "Tell you what. You look around for the forms and stuff that go with the candy, and I'll help you figure out what kind of records to keep till Vickie gets back to finish it all up for you. Does that sound fair?"

Jesse didn't like the direction this conversation was taking. He didn't want to keep records. He didn't want to dispense candy to legions of moms or kids. He didn't want to figure out forms. He just wanted to retreat back into the safe world of contract negotiations. Without thinking, he blurted out, "No. I don't think so."

Rennie's clear gray eyes shot sparks. "What don't you think? You don't want to keep records, you don't want to dispense candy, or you don't want my help?"

Knowing he'd made a grave tactical error, Jesse tried to retrench. "Rennie, I'm sorry. Of course I want your help. In fact, I'd love to spend the next two weeks with you until Vickie gets back."

Rennie jumped to her feet "I cannot believe what I'm hearing. Vickie's hardly out of the house, the girls are just on the other side of that door, and you're coming on to me. If I wouldn't have to answer to the girls, I'd be very tempted to slap your face, *Mr. Daniels!* Now, if you'll excuse me, I'll get out of here before I give in to the temptation."

For a moment, Jesse was stunned by the magnificent sight of Rennie in all her glorious outrage. Realizing she was going to make her exit before he found out why the fact he found her attractive upset her so, he sprang into action. He caught up with her before she reached the front door and grabbed her arm. "What is wrong with you, woman? Have I grown two heads or something? Most women I know would be glad to spend time with me."

"Well, if that's the kind of women you know," Rennie snapped as she jerked her arm free from his grasp, "I don't know whether I feel sorrier for you or for them!"

Jesse trapped her against the front door with one hand on the wall to each side of her shoulders. Even when she was fighting with him, he was aware of his growing attraction to her. The expression in her eyes spoke volumes—and not a word of it complimentary. His gaze was drawn downward to her chest as she took deep breaths to control her temper.

"Let me out of here!" Rennie whispered harshly after watching the trail his eyes followed. "You may not care what the girls think, but I, for one, don't want them to come in here and catch us in this position."

Jesse couldn't resist baiting her some more. "Oh, and just what position would you like them to find us in?" He tried to look innocent as he spoke but failed.

Rennie knocked his arm out of the way and whirled away from the door. "You're really disgusting. If you don't let me out of here pretty damn quick, I swear you'll pay for it dearly."

Jesse held up his hands in a sign of surrender. "Okay, Rennie, I'll back off. I don't usually have to resort to my caveman act until at least the third date." He smiled, trying to lighten the situation. "Look at it like this: You've already got that out of the way."

Before Rennie could respond, Lexi popped out of the door from the kitchen and headed for the stairs up to her room. She stopped when she saw the two adults standing in the foyer glowering at each other. Puzzled, she asked, "Is something wrong, Uncle Jesse?"

Jesse started to reassure her that everything was fine, but Rennie didn't give him a chance.

"Did she say *'Uncle Jesse'*? You're their uncle?" She instinctively stepped back but found herself up against the door again, her back literally to the wall.

Two

Now Jesse was completely baffled. Surely the woman knew what an uncle was. "Yeah, I'm their uncle. Their dad is my older brother, Mark. That's how these things work, you know." He leaned against the wall, his hands in the front pockets of his button-fly jeans. He continued talking slowly and clearly as if explaining a new concept to a very small child. "If someone's brother or sister has kids, that automatically makes them an uncle. Or an aunt in some cases."

"You're their uncle," Rennie repeated, more calmly this time.

"Is that a problem for some reason? Who did you think I was?" Jesse asked.

"No, no problem." Rennie shrugged, then looked at Lexi. "Don't let us keep you, Lexi, if you need to head upstairs for some reason." She smiled, trying to reassure the girl that everything was all right.

"Okay. Good night, Mrs. Sawycr. I've got to get my shower before Brittany hogs all the hot water." Lexi ran up the stairs and disappeared into her room.

Rennie reached for the knob and started to open the front door. "I'll be going now, Mr. Daniels. If you decide that you need help with the candy, please do call me. I know that Vickie's got my number, and I'm in the telephone book, too."

Before she could make her escape, Jesse reached out and shut the door again. "Do you want to explain now why my being the girls' uncle seemed to upset you so? I'd really like to know."

Rennie couldn't look him in the eyes. "Well, you see, I thought you were their father."

"So?" Jesse prompted when she quit talking.

"Vickie's husband."

"So?" he repeated.

This time she blurted out what he was waiting to hear. "So I thought that even though you were married to Vickie, you were coming on to me." She glanced furtively at his face to see his reaction.

"I see," he drawled, a smile tugging at his mouth.

"If you do see, you're seeing me very embarrassed. Now will you please let me out the door before I do anything else to humiliate myself?" Her eyes were huge and nervous-looking.

Jesse moved as if to touch her face, but evidently thought better of it. His voice was soothing, with a slightly husky note when he spoke. "It's okay, you know. It's my fault, too. I should have introduced myself more clearly when we met. Come on, I'll see you to your car."

"No need. I walked." She reached for the door again.

"Wait here a sec so I can tell the girls where I'm going, and I'll walk with you," Jesse offered as he headed for the kitchen.

"Really, Mr. Daniels, it's only a few blocks. I'm a big girl and I can find my own way home."

"My pleasure. By the way, my name is still Jesse," he reminded her as he slipped on a lightweight, dark blue nylon jacket.

Rennie gave in and accepted his offer of escort. "Thanks. To be honest, as quiet as this area is, I still don't like walking alone after dark." She waited out on the porch while he locked the door.

When he joined her, they stepped down off the porch together and turned toward the driveway. Rennie stopped to zip up her jacket and turned her collar up because the temperature had been dropping since the onset of nightfall. A slight fog was gathering in the hollows, shrouding the streetlights in a gentle mist.

Jesse spoke first. "I'm really sorry we got off to such a rocky start. It just never dawned on me that you had me confused with Mark. I assumed that since you knew Vickie, you knew Mark as well. Would it be okay if we started over?"

"Start over?" Rennie asked.

"Yeah, like at the beginning." Jesse's dark eyes gleamed in the yellow moonlight. The shadows of the night emphasized his high cheekbones and finely chiseled nose.

When he grinned at her, she felt it all the way to her toes. He was simply gorgeous, the type of man who spoke directly to her hormones. When she realized she was staring, she looked away quickly and answered, "Sure, let's."

He gravely held out his hand, enveloping her small one in it. "Hello, I'm Jesse Daniels. Lexi and Brittany are my nieces, my brother Mark's girls. I'm not married. I've never been married."

Rennie, in the spirit of the moment, answered with great solemnity. "Hello, I'm Rennie Sawyer. Becky is my daughter and Brittany's best friend. I'm very pleased to meet you."

Jesse had to know. "And are you married? I'm sorry, I don't know why I assumed you weren't, but I did. Do I need to apologize for that, too?" He also didn't know why he had his fingers crossed that she wasn't.

"Not recently." The clipped tone of voice told him that no further questions on the subject would be welcome.

Jesse gave her a reassuring smile, took her by the arm, and headed up the street. In just minutes they reached her home, a small rambler on the next block over from where Mark and Vickie lived.

They walked to the front steps, and Jesse stood back while Rennie located her keys and pulled them from her purse. He took them from her hand, then reached around her to unlock the door, making her intensely aware of how tall he was. "If you'd like me to, I'd be glad to come in and check for things that go bump in the night, Rennie."

"No, that's okay. I'll be fine, and besides, you probably need to get back to the girls." Rennie smiled shyly, her feelings equally divided between wanting to drag Jesse inside and keep him to herself and wanting to distance herself from the man to whom she felt a disturbing attraction.

"If you really meant what you said earlier about helping me, I'll look for the candy papers tomorrow and see what I can figure out. If I need help and you have time in the afternoon, maybe you can show me how to get it all situated." Then he added with that bone-melting grin, "Unless, of course, you want to take pity on a poor bachelor uncle and let me bring all the candy over here?"

"No way! Consider it a learning experience," she laughed. "Call me tomorrow if you need the help. Otherwise, I'll probably see you tomorrow night at the band concert at the elementary school."

Jesse groaned. "Band concert? I suppose it's too much to hope for that this is a professional group playing?"

"Fat chance! The intermediate orchestra is performing, as well as the first-year band. Brittany plays in one and Lexi in the other."

Jesse shuddered, but then threw back his shoulders. "I'm tough. I can handle it." He looked wistful. "I suppose earplugs are bad form."

"You bet they are. You know, Vickie is one of my best friends, and while I wouldn't want to cast any aspersions on your brother and sister-in-law, don't you think this last-minute trip is a little suspicious? First, they're missing the candy sale, and now you find out they're ducking out of town just in time to miss the first band concert of the year." Rennie was laughing up at Jesse's face.

He appeared to give it some serious thought. "I can't think of anything I've ever done to make them hate me that much. You don't think they're just now getting even with me for tagging along on their honeymoon? Naw, that's just too far-fetched."

"You went along on their honeymoon?" Rennie asked incredulously.

"Yeah, I was living with Mark when they got married. He had taken me in when Mom left." Jesse's eyes turned bleak. He hadn't meant to admit that his mom had cared so little about him, but Rennie made it so easy for him to talk. He looked away and said, "Let's get back to better topics."

Recognizing his reluctance to talk about his family, Rennie let him change the subject. "What's a better topic?"

"Well, for instance, when can I see you again?"

Surprised, she said, "Well, I thought we were doing the candy stuff tomorrow." Surely he didn't mean a date, but that's sure what it sounded like.

"No, let me rephrase that. I, Jesse, would like to see you, Rennie, sans kids, for dinner one night. Is that clearer?" His mouth curved in a slight smile, one dark eyebrow arched quizzically.

"Yes, that's clearer, but I don't think we should." She hoped he didn't notice the slight tremor in her hands or perceive the staccato beat of her heart.

"And why not?"

"Well, for one thing, I don't date much." And lately not at all, she added to herself.

"Fine, I like a woman who's selective, especially if she is selecting me." Jesse wasn't giving in easily. He didn't want to analyze his feelings, but suddenly it was very important for him to see Rennie again. And soon.

"This is moving much too quickly for me, Jesse. Let me think about it. Okay?"

"Okay, I guess," he said, his eyes narrowing. "But while you're at it, think about this."

Before Rennie could react, Jesse had his arms around her, pulling her in close to his chest. He tilted his head and leaned down, his intent to kiss her as clear as if he'd announced it. She opened her mouth to protest, but he used that as an opportunity to deepen the kiss immediately.

Rennie didn't think she could move, but somehow her arms found their way up around his neck. Her traitorous body leaned in closer to his. Her mouth welcomed the taste of his lips and then his tongue. Her breath came in ragged gasps, matching the irregular rhythm of his heartbeat that she could feel through all the combined layers of their clothing.

The sound of a car coming up the hill penetrated Jesse's thoughts just before it did Rennie's. With reluctance, he softened the kiss and drew back from the edge of insanity. Insanity, because if the car hadn't interrupted them, he was afraid he'd have done his best to drag her inside the house and finish what they'd started, even if it was on the floor just inside the door. However, he was sure Rennie wasn't that kind of woman. Even if she could have forgiven him, he doubted she would have easily forgiven herself.

He smiled down at her, his voice shaky. "Well, I guess I gave both of us something to think about. Like maybe taking a cold shower."

He could tell she was already having second thoughts. "Look, Rennie, we're both grownups. It's normal for two adults who find each other attractive to enjoy a kiss. And believe me," he said, leering playfully, "I, for one, really enjoyed that one."

As much as she hated to, Rennie couldn't help but return the grin. She had enjoyed the kiss, too, no denying that. In fact, she couldn't remember a kiss she'd enjoyed more. That was what was so scary.

She backed farther away from Jesse's disturbing nearness and stepped inside her house. "Well, thanks for walking me home. You'd better get back to the girls now. Good night." She knew that her rapid speech and rush to close the front door revealed far more of her feelings to him than her words did.

Thankfully, he didn't resist. Jesse simply smiled and stepped away. "Good night, Rennie. And I *will* see you tomorrow."

Rennie didn't miss the emphasis in his last statement. Well, let him think whatever he wanted. Tomorrow, after a good night's sleep, in the light of day, she'd be better equipped for handling the polished charm of Jesse Daniels.

She knew she didn't have what it took to play sophisticated games of flirtation and seduction. They'd been second nature to most of the people that she'd known through her late husband's job as a stockbroker. Sometimes she regretted that she'd been unable to be the kind of wife that Robin had wanted her to be.

Not often, though, because all of the glitz had seemed so shallow, so phony to her. Her only real sorrow was that her inability to fit in with Robin's associates had slowly driven a wedge between her and her husband. In the end, she had sometimes felt like she no longer knew the man she'd married. If a massive coronary hadn't ended their marriage, a divorce would have.

It was too late for recriminations or what-might-have-beens. Robin was gone and nothing would change that. She always tried to remember the good things about their marriage, especially the early days, when they still laughed together. And she still had Becky. In the child, the best of both parents had blended to make a bright and charming little girl. Not so little anymore; she was already eight years old—going on sixteen.

Just then, Rennie heard a car pull into the driveway. Her mother-in-law was back with Becky. Despite her problems with Robin, Rennie had remained quite close to Madeline Sawyer. Since Rennie had no family to speak of, she was especially appreciative of all that Madeline did for both Becky and her. The three women—if she stretched the point to include Becky—did quite well together in their world without men.

She resolutely pushed aside the errant thought that it might be nice to have a man like Jesse in her life. She opened the door to greet her mother-in-law and daughter, hoping that her facial expression didn't reveal her inner turmoil.

* * *

The morning rush was over, and the girls were safely on their way to school. Jesse was out of practice preparing lunches, but he managed to make sure that they had more to eat than the cookies and chips Brittany had tried to tell him was their normal fare. He'd added apples and sandwiches. Of course, that was no guarantee they'd eat anything but the cookies and chips, but at least he'd tried.

The breakfast dishes were rinsed and stacked in the dishwasher. He'd put a chicken casserole out to defrost for dinner. He even had a load of wash running. He was quickly running out of excuses to avoid dealing with the Candy. That's how he thought about it— Candy with a capital C—like it had a life of its own. For all he knew, it could be crossbreeding out there in the garage. If he wasn't careful, they could all be destroyed during the night by a mutant form of chocolate.

He chuckled at the whimsical thought and dutifully reached for the folder he'd found on Vickie's desk that was neatly labeled CANDY DEPOT. He poured himself a fresh cup of coffee, sat down at the kitchen table, and put his feet up on another one of the oak ladder-back chairs.

One page into the information and already his attention was wandering. He looked around the kitchen. This was his favorite room in the house. He'd long ago decided that there was an indefinable quality that some kitchens had that made them the center of a house and transformed it into a home. Vickie's kitchen had that quality in abundance.

The kitchen in his condo didn't have it at all. And Vanessa, a woman he dated only when either of them needed an escort, had every appliance known to modern man. Her kitchen may have an espresso machine, but it didn't have what it took to give her apartment that elusive homelike atmosphere.

Jesse had never been able to clearly define the quality that made Vickie's kitchen different. It wasn't in the clutter on Vickie's built-in desk by the door and it wasn't the new microwave oven. It might have something to do with the artwork and report cards stuck on the refrigerator with a variety of mismatched magnets.

Somehow, Jesse knew Rennie's kitchen always had a jar full of homemade cookies, and her daughter's artwork would be proudly displayed, even if it clashed with the decor. Maybe that's what that elusive quality was—the feeling that people were more important than neatness or style.

Like a child with his nose pressed up against the window of a toy store knowing he had no money, Jesse had the same feeling of longing for something he'd never have. Long ago, he'd accepted the fact that there was some flaw in him that kept him from being good family-man material. So he just hovered around the periphery of Mark's family, soaking up as much of the warmth as he could.

He forced himself to get back to the candy. He concentrated on reading through the forms and the information sheet. Today was Tuesday; that gave him till Thursday to get the candy ready to hand out. If he could get through the half-inch stack of instructions without trouble, maybe he could make some progress on his contract work.

And if he had any questions, well, so much the better. That would give him a perfect excuse to walk over to see Rennie, assuming she didn't work and that she'd be home. She had told him to call her today if he had any problems, so he took that to mean she'd be available.

If not, he could look forward to seeing her later. Tonight was the orchestra concert. He shuddered at the thought.

Rennie wiped the kitchen counter clean, then looked around for something else that needed doing—anything that would keep her hand from reaching for the phone again. Four times this morning she'd found herself in front of her bright red wall phone, itching to call Vickie's number, just in case Jesse needed some help.

Normally, Rennie tried to be completely honest with herself. She'd spent too many years pretending that all was well in her marriage; she couldn't live with self-deceit any longer. It wasn't as if Jesse couldn't handle anything he set his mind to doing. She was just looking for an excuse to see him again, a chance to discover whether the jolt of awareness she'd felt last night would stand the light of day. Maybe it had been only a trick of fiery sunsets and moonlight.

This was silly. Here she was, a grown woman and a mother besides, dithering over a handsome face as if she were a giggly teenage girl. Resolutely, she turned away from the phone, but before she took one step, it rang. She made herself wait till it rang three times before she picked up the receiver.

"Hello," she said softly.

"Hello yourself," a familiar masculine voice came clearly over the line.

"Jesse," was all she could say.

"Good morning, Rennie. Did you sleep well last night?"

"Yes, great," she lied.

"Well, you did better than I did." Jesse chuckled, then lowered his voice until it sounded deep and sexy. "And do you want to know why I couldn't sleep last night?"

"I'd probably be better off not knowing." Damn, she sounded quivering.

"I think I'll tell you anyway, Rennie." He paused, leaving her in suspense. He took a deep breath, then continued, his voice almost a whisper. "I dreamed about us, Rennie. We were alone, just the two of us out in the garage."

"The garage?" she interrupted, leaning against the counter, her legs crossed at the ankle.

"Hush, woman, this is my fantasy, oops, I mean dream. Now let me get on with this. There we were out in the garage. We'd been sorting cases of candy and it was hot. I took my shirt off to cool down, and being the discerning woman you are, you were drawn to my masculine perfection."

Rennie, chuckling at his outlandishness, stopped him for a second. "Let me get this straight. You couldn't sleep because you were dreaming about sweating on chocolate?"

"No, I was dreaming about you being drawn irresistibly to my masculine perfection. Now be quiet and let me finish. You were about to have your wicked, wicked way with me, having cornered me between the peanut brittle and the nut clusters, when Mrs. Billings, leading a troop of commandos, staged a raid to rescue the candy I was holding hostage."

"Commando Trailblazers?" Rennie couldn't hold back her laughter.

"Yeah, they're known and feared worldwide. Don't you keep up with current events? Anyway, heroic figure of a man that I am, I threw myself in front of you to protect you from harm. I got caught in the cross fire and took a direct hit in the chest."

"Oh, Jesse, you dreamed you got shot? No wonder you didn't sleep well."

"No, I got hit with a case of chocolate bars. The whole stack fell in on me. That's when I woke up."

"Well, I can understand that. You weren't having a very restful dream."

Again his voice sounded low and rough, rippling over Rennie's nerve endings, sending shivers up her spine. "The real problem was that I couldn't stop thinking about what would have happened if Mrs. Billings hadn't interrupted us while you were being drawn to my masculine perfection."

Rennie was at a loss for words; she didn't have a clue as to what to say to Jesse. Her mind, however, was working overtime, providing possible endings to Jesse's dream. She would never have thought a garage was a place for dream fantasies, but Jesse's slightly husky voice conjured a picture of broad shoulders shimmering with a fine sheen of moisture, heat generated by the presence of a man, having little or nothing to do with the sun pouring in through the window.

"Rennie, are you still there?" Jesse's voice came through the phone wires, jolting her out of her dream world.

"Oh, uh, sure, Jesse, I'm still here."

"Would you like to know why I really called?"

"Yes, I think that might be good idea."

Jesse laughed gently, almost as if he'd been able to see through the phone lines straight into her mind and the heated visions his words had created.

"I wondered if you could help me get the candy organized this afternoon. I read all the paperwork, and it's all pretty straightforward. I thought if we could divide all the cases for the eight clubs ahead of time, I'd be ready for the onslaught Thursday night. I won't have time tonight to work on it because of the concert at school, and I need at least one day to work on my contracts that I brought home from the office."

Rennie was torn between wanting to be with Jesse again to see if this attraction was real and staying as far away from the handsome charmer as she could. Temptation won out.

"Sure, I'll finish what I'm doing here and be over in about an hour. Is that okay with you?"

"Great! Do you want to do lunch?" Jesse answered.

"I can't believe you just said that!"

"What's wrong with what I said?"

"Real people don't 'do lunch,' Jesse," she primly informed him.

"Real people don't eat?" he asked, truly perplexed.

"Yes, Jesse, they eat. They grab a sandwich, they have a salad, they eat on the run, they grab a bite, they brown-bag it. They absolutely never 'do lunch.' "

"Oh, I see. I bet they don't network either, do they?"

"No one I know has ever networked," Rennie responded, then added, "at least no one I know now . . ." Her voice trailed off at the end, the fun of the game gone.

"Ren, did your husband network?"

"Yes, all the time." Her answer was spoken in a tone that would brook no further questions about the subject.

It didn't matter. Jesse already knew. Her late husband must have been like most of the people Jesse associated with both socially and professionally. They did lunch. They networked. They weren't real, not in any true sense, not in a way that gave a purpose to their lives any deeper than the almighty dollar sign.

Jesse also knew that Rennie would never seek a future entwined with another man like her late husband. He'd only met her once, shared the one kiss, but the realization that his lifestyle would never mesh with hers hurt. It hurt like hell.

This time it was Rennie who wondered if anyone was still on the other end of the phone. "Jess, do you still want me to come over?"

He gave a quick laugh, knowing full well how forced it must have sounded. "How about peanut butter sandwiches and tortilla chips?"

"Only if you have extra chunky," she teased, trying to get past the awkward moment.

"Your wish is my command. I'll have extra chunky or die in the attempt."

"See you in a little while," Rennie said softly into the phone and hung up.

Rennie was bent over, arranging a stack of candy to her satisfaction. Jesse watched her; from behind the view was outstanding. Long legs and gently flared hips only hinted at in the baggy sweats she wore were enticing indeed. He hadn't been this much at the mercy of his hormones since high school. It seemed that the longer he was around Rennie, the more tenuous his control on his reactions became.

It wasn't as if she were setting out to attract him by using artful makeup, designer clothes, or the latest in hairstyles. Her tulip-pink sweats, fresh-scrubbed face, and ponytail were all pushing the right buttons on his libido.

"Hey, Daniels, get back to work. I'm here to help in an advisory capacity only. If you want slave labor, call somebody else." Her expression told Jesse he'd been caught staring at her.

"Sorry, just taking a break." He forced himself to look at something besides Rennie's gray eyes. "Seems like we've about got it licked out here."

Rennie had shown up with some poster-board signs already labeled with the eight club names. They were making short work of dividing the candy according to each club's requirements.

"If I were you, which I'm not," she said with a grin, "I'd start by calling Mrs. Billings to tell her to come get her candy on Wednesday." Seeing his grimace, she added, "Look at it this way, it'll help prevent any commando raids."

"Watch that sassy mouth, woman," Jesse growled back. "This isn't funny—I can face down a hostile jury, take depositions from the meanest of opponents, and even settle out of court, but there is something innately terrifying about marauding candy pushers."

"Get real, Jesse. These are kids just like Lexi and Brittany. By the way, speaking of the girls, have you booked time for them to sell candy at any of the local stores?"

"You mean there was something else they didn't tell me?" He sounded flabbergasted. "I have to call somebody and ask for the privilege of selling candy somewhere?"

Rennie nodded. "Yep, that's where the girls can sell the most candy. It's easier than trying to sell door-to-door." She thought for a second and then said, "Tell you what. I got a block of time at the closest one on Friday night from four till eight. If you're a good boy, I'll share my time."

"What will I have to do?"

"Nothing except show up. The girls will need chairs to sit on and a small table, if you have one. They've done all this before, so they'll know what to do. You just have to stand around, drink coffee, and try to keep warm."

"Will you help me?"

"Keep warm?" she blurted out before she thought.

"Actually," he said, his grin sheer devilment, "while garages full of chocolate may have possibilities, I really don't think standing outside a store with children watching is a proper place for that sort of carrying on."

Rennie punched him on the arm and marched past him into the house. She poured each of them another cup of coffee, adding cream and sugar to hers. When he was finished stacking the last of the candy cases, he came in and sat down at the table. She handed him his coffee and watched as he took an appreciative sip.

How could one man fill up a room? Rennie had been secretly watching him all afternoon when she hoped he wasn't aware of her scrutiny. He was tall enough to make her feel petite and feminine. At five-foot-eight, she rarely met a man who towered over her enough to accomplish that feat.

His well-worn jeans were a designer brand cut to hug his long legs. The faded denim left little to the imagination, especially an overactive one. She'd found her eyes drawn time and again to the open throat of his V-neck sweater and the tantalizing glimpse of muscular chest it revealed.

His hair was a far cry from the neatly styled look of the previous night. One lock had persisted in falling onto his forehead every time he'd bent down to lift another case of candy. Each time he'd run his fingers through his hair, trying to tame the recalcitrant lock. Instead, he gave his hair an appealing, rumpled quality that made Rennie want to brush it back for him and feel its texture for herself.

"I guess I'd better be going, Jesse. The girls are due home from school soon, and I always try to be home before Becky gets there."

Jesse stood and walked to the front door with her. "I really appreciate all the help, Rennie. I'm not very experienced in all these child-related activities."

"No problem. I enjoyed it." She stepped out onto the porch. "I'll be seeing you later, then."

"Later?"

"You know, the concert."

Jesse looked sheepish. "Sorry to be so thickheaded. I think psychologists call it denial."

"Actually, I think you'll be pleasantly surprised at how good the orchestra sounds. All the strings blend together rather nicely."

He pounced on the fact she hadn't mentioned the other half of the scheduled entertainment. "And what about the band?"

"We parents usually refer to it as the individual competition."

"I don't get it."

As Rennie started down the sidewalk to the street, she called over her shoulder, "You will tonight."

Jesse was sure he didn't like the wicked smile she flashed him just before she turned away. The woman really had a sadistic streak that would bear watching. He walked back into the house and checked the time. Lexi and Brittany should be hitting the end of the street in a few minutes.

Thinking back to his own school days, Jesse figured that if the girls were anything like he'd been, they'd be hungry as soon as they came in the door. He decided to have a healthy snack waiting for them rather than facing demands for sweets and junk food.

About the time he'd peeled two oranges and sliced an apple, he heard the girls come in the front door.

"I'm in the kitchen, kids," Jesse called out.

Brittany reached the kitchen first. "Hi, Uncle Jess. Can I have some cookies?"

"Nope, have some fruit. It's all ready to eat."

She looked betrayed. "I thought you told Mom you were here to spoil us. Mom makes us eat healthy junk, too." Nevertheless, she accepted the plate of fruit and sat down at the table.

"Homework tonight?"

"Just some more math," she answered between bites. "I'll do it before dinner because I have to be at school by six-thirty to get ready for the concert."

Jesse was confused. "Did your mom write the time down wrong for me? I'd have sworn the concert started at seven-thirty." Jesse headed for the clipboard full of Vickie's notes and instructions.

Lexi came through the door in time to answer. "Yeah, that's when the concert starts, but the orchestra kids have to be there an hour early to get their instruments tuned by the teacher. Keeps them from sounding so horrible."

Brittany stuck out her tongue at her sister.

"Now, Lexi," Jesse admonished, "no one is going to sound horrible tonight."

She just gave him one of those looks that kids have been giving adults since the beginning of time and dropped her books on the table.

"I'll leave you to your homework," Jesse told them. "I'm going to use my laptop and try to get a little work done before dinner."

"Uncle Jess, where are we eating tonight?" Lexi asked, sounding hopeful.

"Here at home, you minx. If you think I'm taking you out every night and then have to explain to your mom why the freezer's still full of her home cooking, you're nuts," Jesse said laughing. "We'll have chicken casserole at five-thirty. That'll give us time to get the kitchen clean before we head out for the school."

He set the temperature on the oven and put the covered casserole in before leaving the room. "If either of you need any help, yell. Otherwise, I'll be pounding on my computer keys."

Jesse gathered the things he needed and sank down on the couch in the living room. After pulling the coffee table closer, he propped open his briefcase and began arranging stacks of papers in neat piles around the table. He set up his laptop computer and attempted to work. When he couldn't think of anything to write, he tried proofreading the papers he'd already finished at the office.

After about fifteen minutes of intense effort, he couldn't remember a single word he'd just read. He just couldn't keep his mind on the contracts. Clear gray eyes and a bouncing ponytail kept clouding his vision.

Disgusted, he finally threw the papers back into his briefcase and slammed the lid down. He'd never get anything accomplished this way.

What was there about Rennie Sawyer that drew him so?

If he was honest about it, Vanessa Gilbert with her cool sophistication was far more beautiful than Rennie. But then, "cool" was the operative word with Vanessa. The only thing Jesse ever saw Vanessa passionate about was the pursuit of her career goals. She wanted to be a partner in the firm before turning forty. Vanessa quickly, ruthlessly dispensed with anything or anyone who interfered with that goal.

Until now, she'd been the perfect companion for him. She liked to be seen in all the right places, she shied away from anything that hinted at long-term commitment, and together they made an attractive couple. That had been enough.

But having met Rennie, it was like comparing a photo of what a woman should be with a real, live, warm female. Jesse knew he was being unfair to Vanessa. He'd never asked her for more than a casual involvement. But Jesse had been intensely aware of Rennie from the beginning, reacting to her on several levels at once.

She had a clean, wholesome beauty that didn't rely on hours spent in a salon or in front of a mirror. Her eyes reflected a world of living in their silvery depths. When she laughed, her eyes smiled. When she was angry, the sparks flew. And when she was thoroughly kissed, they turned smoky and heavy-lidded.

Rennie was a woman who should send Jesse bolting for the door. She made a man think about home and hearth, about coming home at night to hot meals, warm hugs, and happily-ever-afters. Trouble was, Jesse wasn't the type of man women stayed with for the long term, not even his own mother. If he let himself become too involved with Rennie's warmth, he could guess how he'd feel when she left. Cold. Cold and alone.

Three

Grade-school gyms hadn't changed in the years since Jesse had last been in one. Bulletin boards were cluttered with pictures of how jumping jacks and deep knee bends were properly done. The names of kids with the fastest times, most jumps, most volleys, or best whatevers were written on poster-board lists, proclaiming their skills to the rest of the student population.

For the occasion, the basketball hoops had been raised up out of the way and the rope climbs were tied back. Row upon row of green plastic folding chairs were arranged to face the school stage at one end of the gym. Brittany was already in a long line of students patiently waiting for the orchestra teacher to tune their instruments.

Lexi had run off to visit with friends, leaving Jesse to entertain himself. He chose seats in the third row from the front and sat down. He laid his coat across several of the chairs to save seats not just for the girls, but also for Rennie and Becky. He'd need Rennie's support, he feared, to get through the next couple of hours.

Jesse knew the instant Rennie walked in the gym door. He hoped he wasn't drooling, but the outfit she had on was enough to try the good intentions of a saint. He was sure she didn't realize the effect she had on him; in fact, if she had any inkling, she'd stay as far away from him as she could.

Rennie had pulled her gleaming dark brown hair back with a pair of combs, letting it tumble down to her shoulders in a riot of soft curls. She was wearing soft pink lipstick and just a touch of eye shadow.

Her white jumpsuit was worn off the shoulder with elastic forming soft gathers across the top. Just below the gathers was a lace insert, giving tantalizing hints of the silky skin underneath. Long sleeves ended in elastic cuffs as well. White slip-on sneakers completed the outfit. She wore no jewelry other than some white hoop earrings.

Jesse stood as she approached, smiling in welcome. If his smile was a bit wolfish, he could only hope that Rennie wouldn't notice. As she drew closer, though, her expression began to look a little skittish. Jesse stepped forward to intercept her before she could decide to sit elsewhere.

"Rennie, I'm glad to see you. As you can see, both girls have deserted me." Jesse turned to the small girl holding on to Rennie's hand. "You must be Becky. Brittany told me to tell you to meet her up on stage as soon as you got here. She's already there standing in line."

Becky smiled shyly at Jesse and headed for the stage with her violin in hand. The two girls had promised each other they'd share a music stand for the performance. Jesse had chosen seats that gave the best view of them both.

"Good seats, Jesse."

"Thanks. I sort of hoped you wouldn't mind sitting with me. And the girls, of course," he hastily added. "I don't know another soul in the whole place, and I'm definitely feeling a little out of my element."

Rennie didn't think he looked out of place. His russet pullover sweater brought out the red highlights in his hair rather nicely. Besides, she liked the way he'd pushed up his sleeves, revealing very masculine forearms. The pleated gray cotton pants seemed comfortable, and his light gray leather loafers completed the overall look of casual elegance.

"I'd be delighted to join you, kind sir. Especially since I wouldn't miss the chance to watch you enjoy your first band concert of this caliber for anything." Rennie gave him another one of those vicious grins.

"Do most folks know you have this mean streak in you, Rennie?" He laughed good-naturedly. "I may need to have a talk with Vickie when she gets back about the type of person she's entrusted her daughter to in Trailblazers."

Rennie leaned close to Jesse, giving him a tantalizing whiff of a subtle floral perfume. "Let you in on a secret, pal. Most folks are so glad when someone volunteers to take on a club, they wouldn't care if the last reference she had was from Attila the Hun."

He laughed and casually put his hand on the middle of her back, gently guiding her into the row of chairs. It was all he could do to not bury his face in her hair and take a deep breath of her enticing feminine scent.

Rennie stepped quickly past Jesse and sat down next to him. She could still feel the warm imprint of his hand on her back even after he'd taken his hand away. The soft cotton of her jumpsuit did little to insulate her from the heat of the man next to her. Or maybe she was the one who was hot. No way for a mother to be reacting in the grade-school gym. But then, she didn't feel motherly around Jesse.

"Did you call Mrs. Billings? If not, she'll probably be here tonight so I can introduce you." Rennie stifled a laugh when she saw the panic on Jesse's face. "She won't bite, you know."

"Please, have mercy. I promise I'll call her tomorrow and let her have her candy."

"Well, I guess you have enough to face tonight without adding a commando leader." Rennie grinned up to him. "By the way, when do you want me to pick up my candy?"

"You, I'll let in anytime. In fact, play your cards right and I'll deliver."

Before Rennie could answer that, the orchestra teacher walked to center stage, signaling to the kids to take their seats and come to order. While she made a last few adjustments in tuning, the school principal made some brief announcements. Lexi slipped into the seat next to Rennie just as an honor guard carried in the American flag.

As the entire audience stood for the Pledge of Allegiance, Jesse glanced over to Rennie and then to Lexi. For a few minutes, he let himself pretend that both the woman and the girl were his and together they were a family. Then he told himself that the funny feeling in his stomach and the burning in his eyes were because he always got emotional singing the National Anthem during the flag salute.

Rennie turned to tell Jesse something about the program, but he had such a strange look on his face that she chose to wait. She returned her attention to the orchestra teacher, who was introducing the program.

On cue, thirty beginner string-instrument students raised their bows and the music began. Jesse was impressed. Miracle of miracles, they all managed to start on the same beat. He could even recognize the Mozart tune.

He watched Brittany and Becky as they frowned in concentration on the notes. He had to admit that they'd evidently worked very hard to prepare for the performance. The five songs on the program were finished in short order. All in all, it was fun to hear what the kids could do.

"See," Rennie whispered, "I told you the orchestra sounded pretty good."

Jesse leaned around Rennie to Lexi. "Is it your turn, honey?"

"Yeah, Uncle Jess. The orchestra kids are moving their junk out of the way and then we can go up. It'll take a few minutes to get everything organized. Wish me luck." With that, she was up and heading for the cluster of band students already gathering by the stage steps.

Brittany and Becky ran up and accepted Jesse's congratulations as their just due. They were more interested in getting permission to sit in the back with a bunch of their friends.

"What do you think, Rennie?"

"Go ahead, girls. Just remember to give the band students the same courtesy they gave you," Rennie admonished. "Keep it quiet back there."

Suddenly, Jesse realized he didn't know what instrument Lexi played. He asked Rennie.

Her mouth quirked up on one side. "Guess!"

"Don't tell me—the tuba."

"No, luckily for Vickie," Rennie whispered, her eyes crinkled in amusement.

"Drums? Trumpet? Flute?"

"Wrong, wrong, and still wrong. Speaking of flutes, though, are they called flutists or flautists?"

"Neither," Jesse asserted haughtily, his dimples belying the tone of his voice. "Everyone knows they're called fluters, except when they're this young. Then they're called flutlets. Don't you know anything about music?"

"Excuse me and forgive my ignorance," Rennie replied archly. "You still haven't guessed what Lexi plays."

"A clarinet?"

"Nope, a saxophone." Rennie's smile was wicked.

"All right, woman, out with it. What's so funny about that?"

"You mean that you don't mind that your niece has become a sax offender?" Rennie started giggling.

Her outrageous pun had caught Jesse so unaware that he was unable to hold back a loud laugh. The band teacher was still trying to organize her group and looked around to see what was so funny.

"A sax offender! Woman, you are really bad."

Rennie added one more for good measure. "Yup, and if she takes good care of her instrument, she's a sax therapist."

Other parents were starting to glare at the snickering pair. Both struggled for control and finally managed to maintain serious faces, as long as they didn't look at each other. Finally, the band teacher introduced her half of the program.

With a lift of her baton, the kids in the band quit warming up and held their instruments at the ready. The teacher gave them a four count and then the first notes of "Down on the Farm" rang out over the gym.

Unlike the strings in the orchestra, the various horns and wood-winds could be heard individually—each squeak, each note. Still, for a first-year band, the melody was still recognizable.

"Watch their feet," Rennie whispered near his ear.

The feel of her warm breath on his neck almost kept him from understanding her words. He watched the band members diligently keeping time, only to realize that no two of them were hitting the beat at the same time. He gave Rennie a rueful smile. Considering everything, the kids were making a valiant effort.

Then the solos began. Jesse felt sorry for the one boy whose duet partner was out sick. When a small girl in the back had her flute come apart in her hands, everyone waited patiently and then applauded when she calmly fixed her instrument and bravely continued to perform. Jesse was quite sure that at age eleven, he'd never have been able to handle the same situation with such aplomb.

Soon after, the band finished up its last piece and the concert was over. Much to Jesse's surprise, he found that he'd really enjoyed himself. He knew that largely his pleasure was due to Rennie's presence, but seeing his nieces and their friends working so hard on their music was an important part of the evening's fun as well.

Reluctant to let the night end so early, Jesse waited until the three girls collected their instruments. Then he asked, "Anyone on for ice cream besides me?"

The suggestion was an instant success.

"Can I have an ice cream sundae, Uncle Jess?" Brittany whooped.

"I want mine to be hot fudge," Lexi added, not to be outdone.

When Becky didn't put in her order right away, Jesse asked her gently, "And how about you, young lady? What would you like?"

Becky glanced up to see what Rennie was thinking before answering. When Rennie nodded her encouragement, Becky answered, "I want a German chocolate swirl."

"Well, three decadent concoctions it is, ladies," Jesse agreed and shepherded them all toward the exit.

The three girls ran toward Jesse's car. Realizing that Becky wanted to ride with her friends, Rennie turned to Jesse, "Is it all right if my daughter rides with you? I can follow you."

"Sure, but why don't you ride with me as well? I'll bring you back to pick up your car. We have to come right by here on the way home."

"Okay. It's locked up, so it should be safe enough," Rennie answered. She hesitated briefly before continuing. "By the way, Jesse, I know you meant well to reward the girls' hard work with a treat, but next time I'd appreciate it if you asked me first. If for some reason we couldn't have come, it would have only disappointed Becky."

"Sorry, I did it without thinking. To be honest, I was having such a good time with you and the girls, I wanted to prolong the excursion."

His smile was such a heart stopper, Rennie found it difficult to catch her breath. Luckily, he had to turn his attention to his nieces right then.

He opened the car doors, first for Rennie, and then for the three girls. He climbed in and started the motor. The car purred up the steep hill to the restaurant.

In short order the girls were sitting around a table eating their ice cream with gusto. Rennie had settled for a chocolate cone, but Jesse ordered a wild concoction that had ice cream, hot fudge, peanuts, and whipped cream. The girls insisted on sitting alone, so the two adults chose a booth nearby.

"If I ate something like that, I'd have to diet for two weeks to make up for it." Rennie watched Jesse digging into his ice cream with fiendish determination.

"Nonsense. I specifically told them I wanted this without calories."

"I suppose they also left out the cholesterol?" she asked.

"Yeah, and the sugar, too," Jesse added smugly. "Besides, one reason I put a lot of salt on my food is to keep my blood pressure up high enough to metabolize all the sugar I eat."

At Rennie's horrified gasp, Jesse started laughing. "Seriously, I rarely eat desserts at all, but once in a while I have to cut loose and really indulge myself. I can't remember the last time I had something this decadent."

"I'm glad to hear that. I was about to dust off my old lectures on proper diet and exercise."

"No need. I know all four major food groups and try to make sure I have some of each every day."

Rennie nodded her approval.

Then he continued. "Yep, salt, sugar, additives, and preservatives—got 'em covered." He cracked up when he saw the look on Rennie's face. Before she could say anything, he pointedly eyed her figure. "You don't seem like dieting is a problem for you, though."

"I cook healthy foods for Becky and me because eating habits are learned early. With our family history, it's best for Becky to start out right now."

"Does heart trouble run on your side of the family or on your husband's?"

"His mainly, but my folks had hypertension, too. Robin's dad died of it." Her voice dropped almost to a whisper when she added, "Robin, too. He had a fatal coronary at age thirty-four."

"Did he have any warning that something was wrong?"

"If he did, he never told me." Rennie hesitated, unsure why she wanted to confide in the man across from her. "By that time, we were just sharing a house, not really living together." She glanced at her daughter, the threat of tears burning her eyes. "The real tragedy was that we hardly missed him when he was gone. If that seems cold, I'm sorry, but our paths rarely crossed, and when they did, we just fought."

Jesse reached over and placed his hand over Rennie's. "I'm sorry, honey. I didn't mean to lead the conversation into painful subjects."

She reluctantly pulled her hand away from his and the warmth that it had offered. "That's all right, Jesse. It's all water under the bridge." To lighten the moment, she stole his spoon and took a big bite from his ice cream.

"Hey, stop that. You can't rob a man of his hard-earned pleasures." He lunged for his spoon but only succeeded in knocking some of the ice cream off onto Rennie's lap. She yelped and dropped the spoon. The rest of the melting mess splashed up on her chest. Without thinking, Jesse grabbed some napkins and tried to wipe the dripping chocolate off of her.

Rennie fought down the immediate urge to slap his hand away. She knew he was just trying to repair the damage, but she was uncomfortably aware of each swipe he made with the napkins within inches of her breasts. He was too close for comfort and yet not close enough to satisfy her traitorous hormones. She froze, trying not to breathe.

Jesse finally stopped, crumpling the napkins and dropping them into an ashtray sitting on the table. When he looked up to tell her he'd done the best he could, he saw the strained look on her face. Puzzled at first, it finally dawned on him where his hand had been. He gulped.

"I'm afraid you'll have to wait till you're home to rinse the rest of that out. Sorry about my, uh, I mean your outfit."

"That's okay, Jess. I'm sure it'll all wash out." At a loss as to what she should say next, she looked over to where the girls were sitting to check on their progress. "I guess we'd better be heading on home now. The girls have finished their ice cream and tomorrow is a school day."

Rennie forced herself to look back at Jesse, only to find him watching her intensely. "Is something wrong? I mean, other than my jumpsuit looks like it's wearing the menu."

"No, nothing's wrong, Rennie. You're right, though. We do need to get the girls home and to bed."

Something in his voice didn't sound just right, but Rennie hesitated to press him. Maybe he was just bored with this evening's activities. No doubt, Jesse's normal lifestyle didn't include grade-school concerts and women who manage to spill ice cream on themselves in public. Still, he'd actually seemed to enjoy their shared humor at the poor band's expense. The added trip for ice cream had been his idea, after all.

Shrugging, she scooted out of the booth and walked over to the girls' table. "Okay, time to hit the road. I do want you to know that I'm proud of the hard work you put into the concert tonight. All those hours of practice really showed." Her praise included all three girls, and they were pleased at the compliment.

In short order, both tables were cleared of empty cups, plastic spoons, and soggy napkins. Jesse led the way back to his car. Before he opened the door, he frowned fiercely at the four females and growled, "Whoa, I forgot to check for sticky fingers and grubby mitts. No one gets in Beamer here unless they pass inspection."

Rennie retorted rather tartly, "Tell me something I've always wondered. If this kind of car is so fragile, why do they cost so much?"

Lexi and Brittany, however, recognized their uncle's brand of teasing for what it was and, giggling, held up their hands.

"You two pass." He gentled his expression when he spoke to Becky. "How about you, Miss Sawyer? Any hidden chocolate bits or gooey ice cream waiting to jump on my upholstery?"

After seeing her friends' reactions to Jesse, Becky smiled shyly, holding her hands up for inspection, too. Jesse nodded his approval and let the girls into the back seat.

"Now, woman, that just leaves you." He stepped closer to Rennie and gave her the once-over. "Seems like we have a problem here. I see chocolate sauce and vestiges of ice cream on your uniform." He appeared to give the matter some thought. "Well, I guess as long it's only on the front, it won't get on my car seats." Then he grinned wickedly. "Of course, I do need to inspect your backside, I mean, the back of your outfit to make sure it's safe to let you in my car. I'd hate to have to put you in the trunk or tie you on top."

The girls were laughing at Jesse's antics and at Rennie, who struggled to keep a frown on her face.

"Sir, you leave the back of my clothes alone. I assure you I'm housebroken and am not in the habit of befouling innocent Beamers."

Glancing at the girls, who were watching with great interest, Jesse conceded. "Okay, I'll have to take your word for it this time." Then his voice dropped to a whisper. "Besides, based on my previous inspections, your backside looks just fine."

Rennie glared at her companions in exasperation for having so much fun at her expense. All four of them remained unrepentant, so Rennie swept past Jesse into the front seat of the BMW and buckled her seat belt.

Becky, unsure of her mom's mood, asked from the back seat, "Are you really mad, Mommy?"

Rennie hastened to reassure her daughter. "No, honey, I'm not mad. I've had a lovely time tonight. Just don't tell Mr. Daniels that, okay?"

"Don't tell me what?" Jesse asked as he climbed into the driver's seat.

"It's women talk, Uncle Jess!" Brittany giggled from the back.

"Hey, it's not fair if the four of you gang up on me! I'm just a poor, innocent guy trying to show his ladies a good time." He tried to look crestfallen but failed miserably.

"Well, although women should never let a man feel overconfident," Rennie said, "I guess it wouldn't hurt to tell you, Mr. Daniels, that all of your dates for this evening have enjoyed themselves."

The lights from a passing car briefly illuminated Jesse's face. His eyes were dark and mysterious as he spoke in a whisper just loud enough for her ears only.

"Our next date won't be quite so crowded, Rennie. I want to be able to give you my undivided attention."

Before Rennie could figure out how to reply to that, Jesse was turning into the school parking lot. She decided that her wisest move was to say nothing. He stopped the car just inside the entrance.

Rennie looked at him questioningly. When he didn't say anything else, she asked, "Is something wrong?"

He smiled. "I'm just waiting for you to tell me which car is yours."

"Oh, sorry. It's that van over at the end," she said, pointing across the lot.

Jesse pulled up next to the van. "Seems like a pretty big car for just two people."

"I guess it is more than I really need, but I end up driving the Trailblazers on field trips as well as driving on school outings whenever Becky's teacher needs me. You know, like when the class goes to a play or to a museum."

Rennie realized that she was starting to ramble. After such an easy evening, suddenly she was having a hard time ending it gracefully. Finally, she turned to face the girls in the back seat.

"Lexi, I enjoyed the band's music and you did very well on your solo. Brittany, the strings sounded great. I guess I'll see you at the club meeting tomorrow after school. Becky, thank Mr. Daniels for the ice cream and then we need to get home."

Before she could open her door, Jesse was already out of the car and opening it for her. "You didn't have to get out, Jess," she said.

"I know, but I'm trying to impress you with what a great guy I am." He was smiling, but his tone was unexpectedly serious.

While Becky climbed into the van and fastened her seat belt, Jesse walked around to the driver's side with Rennie. In a quiet voice that wouldn't carry to the girls, he asked, "And how about you, Mrs. Sawyer? Are you going to thank me for the ice cream?"

She dutifully replied, "Thank you, Mr. Daniels."

"Don't I get something better than a few words?"

Her voice turned, sultry and low. "Sure, Jesse, come a little closer."

He took a step nearer to Rennie. Then she surprised him by taking his hand and giving it a firm shake. "Is that what you wanted?"

He glanced over to find his nieces watching the adults with great interest. "No, dammit, it isn't, but considering our audience, it'll have to do." His smile was rueful.

Rennie unlocked the door and opened it. Before getting in, she said, "Thank you again, Jess. Oh, by the way, will you be picking up Brittany after our club meeting tomorrow night or do you want her to walk?"

Jesse couldn't remember seeing anything about that in Vickie's notes. "What does she usually do?"

"Well, if it's dark or raining, Vickie picks her up. Otherwise she walks home most of the time."

"Since I'm only a substitute parent for the next two weeks, I'll play it safe and pick her up." He didn't add that it gave him a legitimate excuse to see Rennie again, however briefly.

"Okay, I'll see you then," Rennie said as she shut her door and started the van.

Jesse returned to his car, trying not to think too hard about how happy he was about seeing Rennie again. Better to concentrate on getting his nieces to bed, and then maybe there'd be time to do some work.

Jesse took off his glasses and closed his eyes for a minute. The specially coated glasses helped prevent eye strain from staring at the computer screen too long, but at eleven o'clock, it was time to call it quits. He'd managed to make some progress on the contracts, but all too often his concentration had been interrupted by thoughts of a certain long-legged lady.

He stretched and rolled his shoulders to relieve the stiffness resulting from typing for the last hour. Leaning back against the couch cushions, Jesse let his thoughts wander.

He'd enjoyed the evening, even the worst notes the kids had hit during the concert. For a few moments, when he'd pretended hard enough, he'd caught a glimmer of what it would be like to be a happily married man. Bright children to nurture and the right woman at his side would bring the completeness to his life that Jesse knew he was missing.

Well, that might be an accurate picture of Mark's life, but Jesse never allowed himself the delusion that it was possible for him. If a man's own mother couldn't love him enough to stay around, there had to be something seriously wrong with him. After all, their mother had been openly affectionate with Mark. On the other hand, when it came to Jesse, she'd always been cold and aloof. For years he'd tried everything he could to please her, but nothing had worked. Finally, after seeing his mother's indifference to his best efforts, he'd decided to find out how she'd handle his worst.

He gave a grin of almost amusement. He'd sure spent a lot of time during his sophomore year staring at the wallpaper in the principal's office. Looking back, he realized he'd never done anything too destructive—he'd acted up in classes, mainly, getting a reputation for being a troublemaker.

His mother had answered the calls from the school with resignation, never seeming to be upset or surprised at anything the authorities said about Jesse. In the end, she'd packed Jesse's bags and driven him to Mark's apartment, thinking if she couldn't handle him, perhaps her good son could. After sulking in his new room for two days, Jesse came out only to learn that his mother had also packed her bags and moved.

Mark had been great. He'd not only dealt with the shock of his mother's disappearance, but with the problems of a rebellious fifteen-year-old as well.

Fortunately for both brothers, Mark was engaged to Vickie. She got more than she bargained for when she married Mark, but somehow Vickie had found it possible to care about the younger brother as well.

All these years later, Jesse had to laugh when he thought about his last outrageous stunt in high school. He'd wired a car horn and an alarm clock to a battery and set the clock to go off about fifteen minutes into the next class period. Then he placed the device in an unused locker and put a heavy-duty padlock on the door. Jesse was sitting attentively in his next class when the horn started blaring.

No one within a hundred feet of the locker could be heard over the noise, even if they shouted. Finally someone thought to track down the janitor to see if he could saw off the lock. All in all, it was a pretty successful prank, considering it disrupted half the school for over forty minutes.

Unfortunately, one of the teachers remembered seeing Jesse in the area of the locker shortly before the class started. With the reputation he'd been getting, he found himself sitting in the principal's office within minutes of the noise being cut off.

Where his mother had never seemed surprised by the damning reports from school, Vickie had looked so hurt when she came to pick him up. Jesse had taken one look at the expression on her face and knew he never wanted to see Vickie so sad again. From that day forward, he'd really cleaned up his act.

Together, Vickie and Mark had always worked hard to make Jesse feel wanted and an integral part of their family. He'd lived with them until he started college.

After that he was with them only for short breaks between semesters. He went to school in the summers, finishing his bachelor's degree in just three years with honors. Law school had come next, followed by a job offer from a pricey law firm that specialized in corporate and contract law.

Now, at age thirty-two, he'd paid off his student loans and was making more than enough money to live comfortably. To pay back

Mark and Vickie for all they had done for him, he'd set up college fund annuities for both Lexi and Brittany.

Everything was going well in his life except for one thing—more and more he was finding that a career and money weren't enough. He wanted a home, not just a place to live. More important, he needed someone to share his life with. Hell, maybe even have a kid. Or three.

That brought back his thoughts full circle to Rennie and her daughter. Shaking his head, he shut down the computer and returned all his papers to his briefcase. After checking the doors, he headed up the steps and made sure the girls were tucked in tight.

He covered Brittany up and turned off the bathroom light that Lexi had left on. Finally, he went into the room that had been his since Vickie and Mark had bought the house. He still had his high school mementos sitting around on the bookshelves and dresser. Although he didn't like to think about it too deeply, he knew the reason was so that he still had a claim staked as part of this household and this family.

He took a quick shower and got into bed. His last thought before drifting off to sleep was to wonder if Rennie could see past the superficial trappings like his car and condo to the real man underneath.

And, like Vickie before her, find something there worth caring about.

Four

Rennie closed her eyes and gently rubbed her temples. After Robin had died, she'd started a home business doing word processing for local businessmen and transcriptions for medical clinics. For Becky's sake, she hadn't wanted to be gone from home any more than necessary, and it was a way to set her own working hours.

All too often lately, when Rennie sat in front of her personal computer for long stretches of time, she developed a severe headache. Maybe she needed to see the eye doctor for some reading glasses. For now, she tried rolling her shoulders to ease the tension and massaged the bridge of her nose with her forefinger and thumb. Neither action did much to relieve the pain that had been steadily worsening for the last hour.

As much as she wanted to finish some work, right now she needed a cold drink and some aspirin. If only she had time to lie down for a short nap, she'd probably feel better. Lord knows she could use the sleep. After spending such an enjoyable evening with Jesse Daniels and his nieces, she'd been troubled with dreams off and on all night long.

The dreams made her restless, wanting something that she'd been without for a long, long time—the pleasures to be found in the arms of a man. And for the first time the man in her dreams wasn't Robin.

No, the man who shared her sleep was very definitely Jesse Daniels, with his brown eyes, long legs, and a smile that made her heart skip a beat each time he unleashed it. The dreams had felt so real that when her alarm went off, she'd been almost surprised that the other pillow on her bed wasn't cushioning his head. And not a little disappointed.

Her subconscious let her fulfill her fantasy of brushing that un-

ruly lock of russet hair back from Jesse's forehead. In her dream
world, she'd tasted his kiss with as much pleasure as when he'd kissed
her the first night they'd met. Her passion was reflected in the heat
of Jesse's brown eyes. Whatever specifics about Jesse Daniels she
was in no position to know had been a blurry haze. That didn't mean
that she hadn't felt his touch and much, much more.

In retrospect, Rennie supposed that a respectable mother, Trailblazer leader, and member in good standing of the PTA should at
least be embarrassed about having such heated, romantic dreams.
Even more so when the object of the dreams was the uncle of her
daughter's best friend. Still, all she could do was smile at the memory.

However, that didn't mean it would be easy to face Jesse Daniels
again. She wasn't sure if she could school her facial expressions to
conceal the questions still reverberating in her mind. Was his chest
smooth? Did the muscles in his shoulders and back really ripple
with such grace and power? Was his— well, she wouldn't let that
question even enter her brain.

Rennie reached the kitchen and headed for the refrigerator. After
surveying her choices, she settled for a diet cola and took a long
satisfying drink with two aspirin. She thought longingly again about
taking a nap. After considering the amount of work she still had to
do, she decided that she'd have to settle for a few minutes' rest with
a warm cloth over her eyes.

Rather than risk the temptation of her queen-sized bed down the
hall, Rennie headed for the couch in the family room, her favorite
place in the house. Robin had insisted on having an interior decorator
select rather formal furnishings for the living room and the adjoining
dining room. Although Rennie thought the furniture was pretty, it
had left her cold—stark reminders of the lifestyle that Robin had
tried to remold her to fit.

In a rare show of stubbornness, Rennie had insisted on picking
out the furniture for the kitchen and family room herself. She'd chosen a casual, comfortable look. A country French table with matching chairs dominated the kitchen. A linen table runner matched the
dark green in the wall paper. The beautifully finished wood flooring
continued into the family room.

The rattan sofa and matching chairs with chintz cushions were
done in myriad colors, brightening the room. Accent pillows lay
about in comfortable abandon. A sturdy coffee table was in just

the right spot for resting tired feet. Large windows added to the bright, sunny look of the room.

With a sigh, Rennie sank into the soft cushions and covered her face with a steamy cloth. Trying to alleviate the strain of her headache, she let her thoughts drift while she waited for the aspirin to take effect. She hoped she would feel better before her Trailblazer club arrived. After a full day of school, the ten girls would be ready for a snack, and then they'd need some time to unwind. It usually took the first thirty minutes of the meeting to get them to settle down to business.

With the candy sale imminent, she planned to review the rules to make sure they understood what they could and could not do. She also needed to remind them that if they wanted to sell candy at any of the stores in the area, they'd better request the time slots they wanted.

And that thought brought her back to Jesse Daniels. She tried to tell herself that she'd invited him to share the time she'd reserved for Becky as a favor to his nieces. She'd be less than honest, though, if she didn't admit that the thought of spending another evening in his company was immensely appealing. After all, the girls needed only minimal supervision, leaving the adults free to talk, share coffee, and, well, just get to know each other.

What an odd thought that was. She'd studiously avoided any romantic involvement since Robin's death. Sure, she'd dated occasionally and friends still tried to fix her up with eligible men once in a while. She'd had no trouble keeping the dates light and friendly— there was never any temptation to let an evening's companionship extend past the front door of her house.

Jesse was the first man she'd met whose kiss left her hungry for more. Even their shared laughter was special. His choice of careers alone should have sent Rennie running for the hills, but the pleasure he found in simple things let him slip past her guard.

She shivered with a sudden chill that wasn't just a draft in the house. If she wasn't careful, Jesse, with his laughing eyes, could hurt her very badly. He wouldn't mean to, of course, but the damage would still be painful. And irreparable.

Her headache had eased somewhat. Besides, she was running out of time before the girls would come blasting through the door with all the giggles and gawkiness of eight-year-olds. She needed to finish up at least two more letters and a medical report before quitting work for the day. Rennie took the now-cool washcloth off her face and sat up. Resolutely, she banished all thoughts of Jesse Daniels from her mind and headed back to her computer.

"Sure thing, Mrs. Billings. I promise I'll call the office tomorrow and see how soon I can get you more candy," Jesse answered, taking a deep breath to control his temper. The woman had been lecturing him for the last ten minutes on the importance of getting a fast start in the candy sales.

"You probably think that I'm just being pushy, Mr. Daniels, but you're new at this. Once you've sold as much candy as I have, I mean my daughter has, you'll understand the importance of—"

"Whoops, is that the phone?" Jesse decided that if he wanted to avoid hearing another dissertation on how to send kids to camp for free, he'd better take quick and decisive action. "Sorry, Mrs. Billings, gotta run." He backed away from her into the relative safety of the garage.

Before she could get another word out of her mouth, he grabbed the overhead door and slammed it shut. He desperately hoped a mere wooden barrier would be enough to protect him from the woman. Briefly he wondered if he was causing any long-term problems for Vickie by being rude to the woman, but he dismissed the thought.

To give credence to his lie in case the woman was watching through the window, Jesse went into the kitchen and picked up the telephone. In all likelihood, Mrs. Billings was outside loading the rest of her candy and getting ready to leave. But just in case, though, he'd better make a call. He turned so his broad back blocked the telephone from view so that he could surreptitiously dial the phone. Without giving it much thought, he dialed Vanessa's direct line at the office.

After two rings, she answered. "Vanessa Gilbert speaking."

"Hi, Vanessa. How's it going?"

"Oh, Jesse." Her voice was carefully modulated to avoid betraying any emotion at all.

Most of the time Jesse didn't mind how cool she was. Today, though, he wished that she could at least sound somewhat pleased to hear from him. After all, they'd been dating on and off for almost nine months. Neither of them harbored any thoughts of emotional entanglements, but still he thought she should sound different for him than she did her for clients.

No, that was ridiculous. Until this week, he'd been just as dedicated to avoiding any awkward involvement as Vanessa was. The difference was a gray-eyed lady who lit up the room when she smiled. After the warmth of Rennie, the chill of Vanessa was harder to take.

"Jess, I'm glad you called," Vanessa said, interrupting his musing. "I need an escort to a cocktail party at the Tower Friday night. It starts at eight. Can you pick me up at seven forty-five, or do you want to meet me downtown?"

When he hesitated before answering, Vanessa broke in with a note of irritation in her voice. "Is there some problem?"

"No. For a minute it seemed like I had something else going on, but I can't think of what it might be. Sure, I can pick you up if that's easier."

They chatted a few minutes more before hanging up. Jesse still had the uneasy feeling that he was forgetting something about Friday, but nothing came to mind. He even checked the calendar and Vickie's notes. Nothing was listed on either for Friday night. He'd have to get a baby-sitter for the girls, but Vickie had left him several names to try.

He still had the vague feeling he was forgetting something, but finally he just shrugged it off. After taking the phone off the hook, he headed for the living room to get started on the final segment of the contract work. He needed to finish before the end of next week and didn't want any unnecessary interruptions.

Hours later he happened to look up from his computer screen and noticed the time.

"Damn, I forgot the girls." He lurched to his feet and took off at a run. Before he got to the door, Lexi let herself in the back door with her key. She was drenched and his heart dropped through the floor.

She started peeling off her soaked jacket and shoes, looking pathetic. "I'm sorry I'm so wet, but when you didn't come, I figured I'd misunderstood and was supposed to walk home."

"Aw, Lexi, I'm sorry. I should have been there, but I lost track of time. You caught me on my way out to get you both." Jesse felt terrible. "Tell you what. You go on up and take a hot bath to get warm. After I pick up Brittany at Rennie's, how about I have a pizza delivered and you can pick the ingredients?"

"That's great, Uncle Jess." She gave the matter some thought. "I want Canadian bacon and pineapple."

Jess made a show of groaning over her choice and then grinned. "I guess I can stomach it. Under the circumstances, I can't complain." He reached for his jacket. "I'll go get your sister. You go get warm."

Lexi disappeared up the stairs and Jesse grabbed a jacket before heading for the door. He'd been so engrossed in his writing, he'd even missed the change in weather. The rain was coming down hard and cold. The trees were whipping around in the wind, and the temperature had dropped at least fifteen chilly degrees.

He reached for the door handle only to hear the phone ring. Lexi must have seen it off the hook and hung up the receiver. Tempted to ignore the shrill noise, he heard Lexi's bathwater running and decided he'd better answer it himself.

"Daniels speaking, " he barked into the receiver.

"Uncle Jesse?" Brittany asked, her voice sounding small and far away. "Should I walk home?"

"No, honey, you just stay at Rennie's. I'll be there in five minutes. Forgive me, pumpkin, but I got buried in paperwork and lost track of time."

"Okay, I'll wait," she answered, sounding very relieved.

Jesse made a dash for his car, cursing the candy that kept his silver baby out of the garage. He hoped that he wasn't wet enough to water-spot the interior, but it couldn't be helped. He had to get to Brittany.

For once he didn't wait for the engine to warm up before driving off. Within seconds he was on his way to Rennie's, hoping he hadn't inconvenienced her too much by his delay in picking up Brittany. He had a feeling that Rennie wouldn't be as forgiving as the girls if she found out that he'd lost himself in a contract to the exclusion of the needs of the two girls depending on him. His total concentration made him a better-than-average attorney, but he doubted she'd find that an appealing characteristic.

He turned into the driveway at Rennie's house. The rain was worse, if anything, so he turned up his jacket collar and ran for the front door. Brittany must have been watching from the front window because she opened the door just as soon as he reached the porch.

"Uncle Jess, I'm sorry for bothering you," she wailed as she threw herself in his arms.

"Brit, you're no bother. This was my fault, not yours." He hugged her close, and then gently wiped the tears off her face with his hand. "Will you accept a pizza apology from your favorite uncle?"

She sniffed. "You're my only uncle."

"See, that means I have to be your favorite." He winked at her.

Brittany managed a smile and hug for Jesse. "I'll get my book bag from Becky's room, Uncle Jess, and then I'll be ready to go." She headed down the hall off to the left.

"Is everything okay?" Rennie's voice came from the kitchen through the open door behind Jesse.

He crossed the living room to find her. "Yeah, everything's okay. Lucky for me both girls are pretty forgiving of their uncle."

Rennie was standing at the stove with her back to him, stirring something that smelled heavenly. A few locks of her hair had worked themselves free from her ponytail. Jesse found himself fighting the urge to brush them out of the way to kiss her long, graceful neck. She turned from the counter to face him before he got carried away.

"Did you have car trouble or something? Brittany was awfully worried." Her gray eyes showed her concern.

"No, I just got into some tricky wording in a contract I'm drawing up for a client and lost track of time." He shrugged. "Next time I'll set my wristwatch alarm to remind me. Sorry if I caused you any problems."

Rennie's eyes narrowed, her voice carefully neutral. "No, you didn't cause me any problems. Except for trying to keep Brittany from calling the police because she knew her favorite uncle wouldn't forget her. She was terrified that you were in an accident or something. Then when we couldn't get through to you, the operator told us your phone was off the hook. Brittany's next thought was that a bad guy, to quote her, was holding you at gunpoint."

She was gripping the wooden-handled spoon so hard that her knuckles were white. She was far more upset about the occurrence than she wanted Jesse to realize. He was feeling guilty enough by himself to react with defensive anger to her scathing comments. He stepped toward her, his eyes blazing. One look at his face and she backed up a step.

"Listen, lady, don't you think you're overreacting? I mean, I admit I should've kept better track of time, but no permanent damage was done. I've already apologized to both Lexi and Brittany and they're fine. What's wrong with you anyway?" He stood ramrod straight, his fists clenched at his sides.

Rennie snapped back, "Nothing. I just have trouble dealing with men that hold pieces of paper to be more important than commitments to people. Lord knows bringing another contract into being far surpasses the needs of two young girls!" She turned away abruptly and jerked the refrigerator door open. After pulling out a head of lettuce, she slammed the door closed.

"Look, I never said the contract was more important than the girls. I'm not used to working my schedule around kids, and I assure you it won't happen again. You might keep in mind that I've been at this less than a week; you've had eight years to learn how to parent."

He quit talking, waiting for Rennie to respond. While he waited, he watched her rip the lettuce into small pieces. "Come on, Rennie, I really am sorry. I'd never hurt the girls deliberately."

Sighing, Rennie looked over her shoulder. "I guess I'm overreacting. Robin used to forget things like this a lot." Closing her eyes in remembered pain, she continued, "Sometimes I think he forgot he even had a home." Sighing, she added, "It's my turn to apologize. I guess I've never gotten over some of my anger with him."

Jesse moved to stand behind her and gently massaged her shoulders. The tension eased gradually, but a different kind was born. "I'm glad we settled that, Rennie. The way you were tearing into that innocent head of lettuce, I was getting worried it was going to literally be a tossed salad—with me as the target."

Rennie managed a chuckle. "Be glad it wasn't a gelatin salad then, because I'll admit the thought crossed my mind."

He pretended to give the matter some thought. "Before I decide which would have been preferable, let me ask this: Were you going to put anchovies in with the lettuce?"

Rennie shuddered in revulsion.

"I guess I can take that as a no," Jesse stated, his brown eyes twinkling in good humor. "You're right, Jell-O would have been worse."

He gently turned Rennie to face him. He lifted her chin, wanting to kiss the last of the sadness out of her gray eyes. Just as he leaned closer to capture her lips, Brittany walked in with Becky right behind her. The two adults jumped away from each other like two teenagers caught necking by the local police.

"Uh, no, Rennie, I don't see anything in your eye. Does it feel better now?"

Jesse doubted the girls were fooled, but he felt the need to save Rennie embarrassment if he could. From what he knew about her, she probably wasn't used to being caught kissing any man in the kitchen by her daughter, much less one whom she'd known less than a week.

"My eye is fine." Rennie made a halfhearted swipe at her left eye. "Thank you for your help, Jesse." Her emphasis on the last statement was to let him know that she'd understood what he was trying to do and appreciated it.

Rennie joined the two girls, draping her arm across Becky's shoulder to reassure her daughter that everything was okay. "Well, Brittany, we sure are seeing a lot of each other this week. I'll probably pick our candy up tomorrow during the day, so I won't see you then, but don't forget we're selling candy together Friday night."

The girls responded with excited comments about how much they'd sell. Rennie had gone over the entire program at their meeting, explaining that they could use their candy credit toward camp fees or to buy stuff at the camp store during the summer.

While they exchanged opinions on the best use of their soon-to-be-earned fortune, Rennie glanced over Brittany's head at Jesse, who was looking like he'd swallowed something particularly vile. The expression was gone so quickly, she almost doubted seeing it. "Is something wrong? We're still on for Friday night, aren't we?"

"Sure, Friday's fine." Before Rennie could ask any more questions, Jesse had Brittany by the hand, urging her to the front door. "Thanks for everything again, Rennie. We'd better be getting back to Lexi."

Rennie was confused by his sudden hurry to be gone when just minutes before his eyes had clearly conveyed his desire to kiss her. For a second she thought she'd misread his intent, but no, the heat of the moment had been unmistakable. She couldn't let him leave without some assurance that everything was okay between them.

"So I'll see you tomorrow, right?" she asked as she followed him toward the door.

"Tomorrow?" Jesse was really looking panicky.

"Yes, tomorrow's Thursday. All the clubs are supposed to pick up their allotment of candy." Her mouth quirked in an almost smile. "You know, all those boxes taking up your Beamer's space in the garage?"

"Oh, that candy. Sure, you can pick it up anytime. With the exception of Mrs. Billings, the other candy folks are coming by in the afternoon."

Rennie smirked. "What did you do—cave in and deliver hers early?"

Jesse paused in the doorway to look back at Rennie. "No, she picked it up this afternoon." He sounded almost defensive.

With that, Jesse was gone, leaving Rennie wondering what had upset him so badly.

Jesse was improving at handling the nightly ritual of getting his nieces to bed. After the first night, they'd found out he wasn't the pushover they had figured on and went to bed at their regular time with a minimum of grumbling. Of course, Lexi had told him rather haughtily that she'd long outgrown the need for bedtime stories. Brittany was good-naturedly letting her uncle read some of his favorite Dr. Seuss books to her each night before turning out the lights.

Once he was sure they were settling in to sleep, he trudged back downstairs, bracing himself for a call to Vanessa. She wasn't going to like it when he told her he'd have to back out on their date for Friday night. Rennie's casual comment about selling candy together that evening had hit him like a blow to the stomach.

He wouldn't have reacted so strongly if he hadn't just spent the last fifteen minutes assuring the woman that he wasn't the type to forget commitments to the girls—or her—regularly. If he'd admitted that he'd made other plans, especially involving another woman, he felt certain her forgiveness would be a long time coming.

While he'd known Vanessa longer, Jesse didn't question why it was Rennie's feelings he was more concerned with. Even so, he 'didn't relish telling Vanessa the bad news. The cocktail party was the place to be to make contacts that could very well advance both her career and his own. Giving that up to peddle candy at the mall would be inconceivable to someone like Vanessa, who pursued her career with single-minded determination.

Jesse carried the phone over to the kitchen table, where he'd set up his computer. Working late was one thing Vanessa would not only understand but would approve of wholeheartedly. Wishing for sudden inspiration, he dialed her number. He let it ring several times, hoping she wasn't home and he could get by with leaving his news on her answering machine.

Finally when her recorded message started playing, he relaxed and leaned back in the chair. After the beeping tone, he spoke, "Vanessa, it's me. I need to talk to you about Friday—"

Before he finished the sentence, Vanessa broke in. "Sorry about the answering machine, Jess, but I was doing some work and wanted to screen my calls. Can you wait a second while I go turn off my printer? It makes it hard for me to hear on the phone."

"Sure." That would give him a last chance to think of a graceful way to break their date.

All too quickly she was back. "Now, what did you want to tell me about Friday night? Do you need to meet me there instead of picking me up at home?"

"No, I can't make it at all. I apologize, Vanessa, but something's come up that I can't get out of." He paused, still at a loss for what to say.

Her voice was definitely chillier. "What's wrong? Just this morning everything was fine."

"I'm really sorry, Van, but I did tell you when you brought this all up that I had a feeling there was something else I was supposed to be doing Friday night." He waited for the explosion.

"Just what is this something else?" Each word was carefully enunciated, betraying no emotion.

He knew then she was really angry. "I've got another commitment. I haven't been into the office all week. You know, I told you I was staying with my nieces while my brother and his wife are in Hawaii. When I called into the office this afternoon, my secretary Sue reminded me of a meeting scheduled from four to at least eight o'clock."

A little more cordially, she asked, "Who's the client?"

Crossing his fingers for luck, he blurted out, "It's a sales meeting with a large candy distributor. We're trying to negotiate production and sales quotas for one of the divisions. If we're successful, it could mean some real perks next summer in the retail market."

That wasn't exactly a lie, he told himself. Brittany and Lexi really could buy sweat shirts at the camp store with their candy credits.

Sacrificing one's personal life for business reasons was something Vanessa understood and approved of. "Well, I'm sorry you won't be there because you'll miss meeting the new partner in our firm. Maybe next time. Call if you need me for anything. Otherwise, I'll take a rain check for Friday night, Jess."

Feeling no little amount of guilt for deliberately misleading her, Jesse ended the call with a promise to be in touch with her soon. Then he sat back and took a deep breath. So far, so good. He wasn't in the habit of being involved with two women at the same time. With the long years of working his way through college and then law school, he'd had little time for socializing.

Since graduation, he'd been concentrating on establishing a successful career, not a thick black book. He had a much better understanding of tort law than he had of the intricacies of male-female relations. In fact, he'd been seeing Vanessa longer than he'd dated any of her few predecessors, and his relationship with her was more convenient than romantic for the both of them.

Then there was Rennie with her gray eyes reflecting so much of what she felt and her easy smile that warmed parts of Jesse that he'd never realized were so cold. Not to mention her long, long legs that continually affected his libido, he thought wryly.

He realized then that he'd been staring at a blank screen on his computer for the last few minutes. If he didn't get some real work done on this contract, he wouldn't have a career left to pursue. He entered a file code and settled in for a long night's work.

Five

Friday morning dawned gray and rainy—a typical Pacific Northwest day. Rennie knew that in other parts of the country, people made concessions to the weather, but in the Northwest, everyone just assumed it was raining without bothering to look out the window and calmly went on with their lives. If it meant jogging in the rain, so be it. It was the price the locals paid for lush lawns, towering trees, and flowers so brightly colored that even the grayest of days didn't dim their beauty.

Rennie stood near her front door doing some leg stretches, waiting for Becky to finish getting ready for school. Three mornings a week, Rennie ran two miles along the roads in the neighborhood. If she timed it right, she could head out in one direction and circle the block just in time to see Becky off at her bus stop down the street. Then Rennie could continue her running knowing Becky was safely en route to school.

"Do you have your lunch, honey?" Rennie asked when Becky appeared.

"Yeah." Becky patted the side of her book bag.

"How about milk money?"

"That, too."

"How about a hug for your mom?" Rennie stood with her hands on her hips, enjoying the familiar game with Becky. She watched while her daughter pretended to check all her pockets and even the zipper pouch on her bag to see if she had any hugs to give away.

Finally, Becky managed to find a hug. "Here's one, Mom." Giggling, she threw herself into Rennie's waiting arms.

"Oh, honey, your hugs feel so good to me." She kissed Becky on top of her dark head. "Better get your jacket on because it's raining a little."

In short order, they both stepped out onto the porch. Rennie locked the door behind them and gave Becky one last hug before setting off down the street in the opposite direction of Becky's bus stop.

Twenty minutes later, Rennie was back on her porch glaring at the door. Self-control was all that kept her from kicking it to vent her frustration. In her hurry to make sure that Becky had everything she needed for the day, she'd forgotten her own keys. So here she was, sweaty, hot, damp from the rain, and no way to get into the house short of breaking a window.

None of the neighbors were home either, so she couldn't borrow a phone to call a locksmith. She didn't have a quarter even if there had been a pay phone nearby, which of course there wasn't.

She took a calming breath, which didn't work, and faced the fact that she'd have to go to Vickie's house and ask Jesse for her spare key. Vickie kept it there for just such contingencies. They'd traded door keys sometime ago when Mark had left while Vickie was out walking, accidentally locking her out of their house.

If Rennie had taken her shower or at least had a comb with her, she wouldn't mind seeing Jesse and maybe sharing a hot cup of coffee. But no, her reflection in the front window revealed all the effects of running in the rain on her appearance. Her hair was so wet it looked almost black. Her sweats weren't a designer brand or stylish. In their heyday they'd been a bright red, but numerous washings had rendered them a faded rose color. A few splashes of muddy water certainly didn't help.

She racked her brain another minute or so, trying to come up with an alternate solution. Finding none, she set off down the street. She hoped that Jesse had a strong stomach and could stand to look at the real, unadorned Rennie Sawyer at nine o'clock in the morning.

Her purposeful stride made short work of the few blocks to Vickie's house. Jesse's beloved car was sitting in the driveway, so it appeared that he was indeed home. Although she didn't relish his seeing her in this bedraggled condition, he was her last hope for getting back into her house without having to start knocking on strange doors until she found someone who was home.

She marched up the sidewalk to the front door and knocked before her resolve wavered. When there was no immediate response, she knocked again. Just before she gave up, she thought she heard Jesse's muffled voice through the door mumble something about holding her horses.

Finally, after a couple of failed attempts to master the dead-bolt mechanism, Jesse succeeded in opening the door. Rennie barely managed to squelch a laugh because from the look on Jesse's face, she was afraid he'd slam the door in her face. Evidently the handsome Jesse Daniels was not a morning person.

" 'Morning, Jesse," she chirped brightly, unable to completely suppress her malicious delight. He looked every bit as bad as she did and he didn't have her excuse of being locked out in the rain.

"What's good about it?" he grumbled back.

"Well, at least you're not locked out of your house like I am." She waited patiently for him to realize he was keeping her standing out on the porch. When he didn't, she added, "Are you going to let me in or not?"

"Yeah, if you promise not to look so happy until I can get a cup of coffee. I can't stand to look at a smile till I'm on my second cup." He motioned her to follow him and led the way into the kitchen.

He was wearing a robe over some disreputable sweat pants that made Rennie's look good. He hadn't bothered with a shirt underneath, and Rennie had caught a glimpse of a very appealing chest. While she'd never liked very hairy men, Jesse had just the right amount of chest hair to make a woman want to run her fingers through it—repeatedly.

After watching him stand in front of the coffee maker looking extremely confused, she took mercy on him and shoved him toward one of the chairs at the table. She made quick work of finding the filters and coffee in the cabinet. In short order, the smell of fresh-brewed coffee was in the air.

"Do you take cream or sugar with your coffee?"

Jesse was leaning back in the chair, his arms hanging slack at his sides, his eyes closed. "Black, very black, if I'm going to get my heart started this morning." He sighed in gratitude when she set the cup in front of him.

"Would you like me to cook you some breakfast or something? You don't seem up to doing much for yourself this morning."

He opened one rather bleary eye and looked at her. "Don't mention food yet, please, if you have any sympathy for a man in pain."

Rennie felt instant concern. "Are you sick, Jess?"

The coffee must have been having some effect because he almost smiled. "No, I'm not a morning person."

"What a surprise!" Rennie teased.

"When I'm at home, I set my coffee maker the night before so when I stumble out of bed into the shower, the aroma alone keeps me going till I reach the kitchen. I'm not used to dealing with cheery kids at the crack of dawn every morning. I worked late last night again and didn't wake up in time to do much more than wave bye at the girls as they headed out the door." He shuddered. "How can anyone giggle at seven-thirty in the morning?" he asked balefully.

Rennie finally gave way to the urge to laugh at the pitiful man in front of her.

"I should have known when you made fun of the band the other night that you had a vicious streak in you, woman. Go ahead and enjoy yourself at my expense, but I'm warning you, as soon as this caffeine kicks in, I'll start planning my revenge." His eyes were fully open now, and Rennie could see the beginnings of humor glinting in their brown depths.

"Now, what was that you said about being locked out?" he asked.

"I left for my morning run at the same time that Becky left for school. In the rush, I forgot my key and locked myself out."

"Serves you right for doing something that disgusting at this hour," Jesse said, smirking. He pushed himself up from his chair and headed for the counter to pour another cup of coffee.

"I suppose that if it's too early for exercise, it's also too early for a lecture on cutting back on caffeine?" Rennie inquired sweetly.

"In this state, that question alone is grounds for justifiable homicide, so watch yourself."

Rennie snorted derisively.

"Hey, I'm a lawyer. I know these things," Jesse assured her, completely straight-faced.

"You told me that you specialize in corporate law, not criminal," Rennie pointed out.

"Well, I wouldn't do it myself, silly. I'd take a contract out on you."

They both laughed. It had been years since Rennie had the chance to enjoy a morning cup of coffee with an attractive man. She'd forgotten how pleasurable it could be.

"Back to the problem at hand, Jess. Vickie keeps a key here for me, but I'm not sure where she has it." She hesitated to start rooting through cabinets without permission.

Jesse thought a minute, his eyes flickering around the room. "I know! There's a rack of keys out in the garage. I bet that's where it is." He opened the door to the garage and leaned out to lift a wooden rack off its hook. He brought it back over to Rennie at the table. "Do you know which one it is?"

Evidently, Vickie kept the extra key collection for the entire neighborhood. Rennie had deliberately had her extra key made in bright red so that it stood out. Unfortunately, several other folks had had the same idea.

"It's one of the red ones." She counted four keys, all the same general shape and color.

"Tell you what. Since you were nice enough to give me a caffeine transfusion, I'll come with you and help you get back into your house."

"Oh, no. I've already bothered you enough for one morning. I'll take the keys and bring them back." She reached for the rack.

Jesse put his warm hand over hers to stop her. Brown eyes smiled gently into gray. "No trouble. Besides, if the keys don't work, you'll need to come back to use the phone."

"That's true. It's just that I feel stupid enough without dragging you out to rescue me."

Jesse revealed his final argument. "Have you looked outside since you got here? If you think you were wet when you came in, the way it's pouring now, you'd be washed down the sewer before you reach the end of the block." He tried to look forlorn, but the gleam in his eyes gave him away. "How would I break the news to Becky? Sorry, honey, but your mom's somewhere in Puget Sound, so dinner might be late."

"All right, all right. No more melodrama please. If you don't mind a rain-splattered desperate person in your car, I'll let you drive me home." She hoped her surrender didn't reveal her very real desire to spend more time in Jesse's company.

"You're finally being sensible. You sit here and enjoy your coffee while I go upstairs and hop in the shower." He picked up the coffeepot and added more to her mug to warm it up. "Help yourself to some toast or something if you want. I won't be long."

In a short time, Rennie heard the shower start running. While she tried to keep her wayward mind on noble, uplifting thoughts, her imagination kept forming pictures of Jesse in all his natural glory. First came images of Jesse removing his robe, leaving his chest bare. The sweats were next to go.

She gave her imagination a stern lecture. Evidently, not stern enough, though, because a vivid image of Jesse standing under the shower spray, his skin gleaming from the steamy warmth, droplets of water shining like diamonds in his hair, popped into her mind. She had to admit, the shower wasn't the only thing steamy in the house.

If this didn't stop, she thought ruefully, she might have to borrow the shower when he was done, but with the water setting on cold. To take her mind off of Jesse's physique, she decided to straighten up the kitchen. She rinsed the girls' cereal bowls and her own coffee cup and stacked them in the dishwasher. She knew better than to mess with Jesse's cup. She was wiping down the counters and the stove top when Jesse returned.

"Hey, you didn't have to do that. I'd have cleaned up the kitchen later."

"No trouble. I wanted to do it." She looked over her shoulder after she answered him. Suddenly she had trouble breathing, much less talking. He was still towel-drying his hair, his shirt on but not buttoned, the top snap of his form-fitting jeans undone, waiting for him to tuck in his shirt. Rennie wasn't sure if she was suffering from a rush of adrenaline or estrogen. Either way, her heart was pounding so loud she was amazed Jesse couldn't hear it.

If she could package this man's sex appeal to sell, she'd be a rich woman in short order. She started scrubbing the counter even harder to work off some of her excess energy.

She felt Jesse's presence behind her before he spoke.

"You might want to ease up or you'll take the protective finish off the wood, Rennie." He paused before asking, "Is something wrong?"

She didn't realize how near he was until she turned around and found herself with a close-up view of his chest. "No," she squeaked. She cleared her throat and tried again. "I'm fine."

She closed her eyes for a second and took a deep breath. It didn't help because now her senses were bombarded with the warm odors of soap and after-shave combined with the male scent that was uniquely Jesse's. Her eyes flew open, meeting his knowing gaze.

He patiently waited to see if she was going to bolt for the door. She didn't. His one hand, almost of its own volition, cupped the back of her head while the other reached around behind her to pull her closer to him. She came willingly into his arms, her face pressed against his chest.

"Rennie." His voice made her name a caress. "Honey, what you do to me when you look at me with such hunger in your eyes." His lips met hers in a gentle greeting.

She sighed in pleasure while giving in to the desire to discover for herself the contrasting textures of Jesse's warm skin and the dusting of hair on his chest. When he sought to deepen the kiss, she didn't just allow it. She demanded it. Would have begged for it if he hadn't made the first move.

His hands moved, too. First to welcome her into his arms, then to familiarize themselves with Rennie's softness and curves. Her height made her a perfect fit, neither too short nor too tall. He lost himself in a kiss he wasn't sure he'd survive.

When the phone rang, it took several seconds before either of them could marshal their thoughts enough to answer it. Jesse got there first, still cradling Rennie in his other arm.

"Daniels here." He couldn't help the sharp tone. He was having trouble breathing much less talking pleasantly.

"Mr. Daniels? It's Sue."

"Sue?"

"Your secretary—you know, the woman who does your typing, answers your phone, that sort of thing." Her statement was punctuated with chuckles. "I know it's morning, boss, but you usually can at least understand simple words."

"Very funny," he growled.

"Seriously, did I call at a bad time? I've got those figures ready that you wanted."

"Let me get a pad and I'll take them down. Hold on for a minute." He laid the phone on the counter and gave Rennie a quick hug. He was afraid she'd skitter off if he let go of her too quickly. "This won't take long, Rennie, I promise."

Rennie stepped away to give him room to write. She watched sadly as he became engrossed in the discussion with his secretary. Intellectually she knew he had to work to make a living. Emotionally, however, she wished that he'd found it more difficult to switch gears. One moment he was kissing her as if it were the most important thing in the world, the next he was immersed in variable interest rates per annum.

When Jesse hung up the phone, he was surprised to see that fifteen minutes had passed since he'd had to let go of Rennie to take the call. He knew instantly it would be impossible to regain the mood they'd shared before Sue had called. Rennie was at the table, idly flipping pages of a magazine. Only the constant movement of her foot revealed how tense she was.

"I'm sorry, Rennie. Sue's a good secretary. I'd hate to fire her for calling at the wrong time."

Rennie's answering smile was weak at best and didn't come anywhere close to changing the bleak look in her eyes. "If you're ready, I really need to get home and get to work."

Jesse pretended to pout. "Some compliment to my ego, lady. Leaving me to rush home and dust."

"I work out of my house. I do word processing for some of the businesses in the area." She stood up, waiting expectantly for Jesse to get ready to go.

He tried to keep the conversation alive. "Have you done it long?"

"After Robin died, I took courses at the junior college. It allows me to work flexible hours, but I still have to meet deadlines."

He was relieved that she didn't pull away when he put his arm loosely around her shoulder. "Well, we'd better see about getting you back in your house, then."

A few minutes later, the fourth key opened her door. "It would be the last one," Rennie complained with some disgust.

"Better than breaking a window," was Jesse's only comment.

Both of them were feeling a little awkward now. Rennie knew it wasn't Jesse's fault that his secretary had interrupted them. In fact, looking back, she was almost glad the woman had called.

"Thanks again for rescuing me. Maybe now I'll finally get around to hiding a key around in back somewhere." She knew her rushed words revealed her nervousness.

"Yeah, well, no bother. In fact, I rather enjoyed myself this morning. That's sort of a novelty for me. It's no joke around my office that if you want a favorable response from me, you'd better wait till after lunch to ask." He grinned unrepentantly.

He gave Rennie a quick kiss on the cheek, nothing that she'd find threatening, just a friendly reminder that he cared. "I guess I'll see you this evening for the kickoff of the great candy sale. Seems silly to take two cars. Do you want me to drive or would you rather?"

"You drove for ice cream. I'll pick you and the girls up in my van. Don't forget warm clothes and hot drinks."

"Great! See you then." He got back into his car. As he drove off, he looked back in time to see Rennie still standing on her porch, her hand on her face where he'd kissed her.

He smiled a very satisfied smile all the way home.

Six

"Hey, Uncle Jess, hurry up! They're waiting for us," Lexi yelled as she went out the front door.

"I'm coming, I'm coming," Jesse grumbled to no one in particular. Both girls had already abandoned him, leaving him to carry their table and chairs out to the car. He hoped they had picked up his Thermos of coffee and the other one of hot chocolate.

The only thing the evening had going for it was the fact that he would share it with Rennie. Somehow, he resolved, he would find a way to have an evening alone with her soon. He might have a hard time overcoming her reservations, but it would be worth the effort. He just knew it.

He stepped out onto the porch and leaned the chairs against his knee while he pulled the door shut, making sure it was locked.

Rennie rolled her window down and called out, "Do you need any help?"

"No, I can manage. Ask the girls if they got the Thermoses in the van for me." After she relayed the question, Lexi held up two red plaid cylinders so Jesse could see that she had them.

He carried the table and chairs over to the back of the van, where Rennie already had the door open and waiting for him. He loaded the gear and then walked around the other side of the van to climb into the passenger seat.

"Does it always take this much stuff just to get kids out the door?" he asked while he fastened his shoulder harness.

"Nope, usually it's worse," Rennie teased. Before she started the van, she smiled slyly. "By the way, are Brittany and Lexi just going to watch Becky sell?"

"No, why?" Jesse was clearly puzzled by her question.

"I didn't see you pack any candy."

"Damn, I knew I was forgetting something," he muttered disgustedly as he unbuckled his seat belt. "Be back in a minute. How much should I bring?"

"I'd say five or six cases total should be enough for the two of them. Bring mostly chocolate bars, though, because they always sell the best."

He unlocked the garage door and lifted it open. In a matter of minutes he had the cases of candy stowed with the table and chairs. Rennie waited for him to get settled again, and then she backed out of the driveway.

"Which grocery store are we going to?" Jesse asked.

"We're not. This year we have permission to sell outside some of the department stores at the mall. We got lucky when I called for a spot. We're selling outside of one of the most expensive clothing stores in the area. We stand a good chance of selling a lot of candy there."

"I never realized how much effort went into organizing something like this candy sale," Jesse said thoughtfully.

"Surely you sold candy or cookies or something when you and Mark were kids."

"Maybe Mark did. I never belonged to anything like Scouts when I was a kid, so most of this is new to me." He sounded determinedly cheerful.

Rennie prompted him when he quit talking. "No Little League or anything?"

"No, my dad died when I was about Brittany's age, so it was all Mom could do to keep food on the table. She didn't have much time left for me . . . I mean, for outside activities." His words were said in an expressionless monotone.

Rennie picked up on the underlying pain in his statement anyway. She didn't want to pry into Jesse's past with the girls sitting right behind them in the back seat. Still, she had a hard time hiding her shock that any mother wouldn't have made time for a son like Jesse.

Tactfully, she changed the topic. "At least it's not raining. Although candy sales seem to be better when you've got the pathetic angle going for you."

That got Jesse's attention. "What exactly is the pathetic angle? That's a new sales technique on me."

Solemnly, she explained. "Have you ever seen kids outside a store selling anything when it's raining? They sit there, kind of hunched up, shivering and miserable-looking."

"Yeah, I always feel obligated to buy from them—more than I usually would."

Rennie grinned triumphantly. "Exactly! We rehearse that whole look. It takes hours of practice, but it really pays off in the end. They can even earn badges if they're good at it."

All three girls started giggling at Rennie's outlandish claim.

Jesse looked over his shoulder, pretending to frown. "Go ahead, make fun of your poor uncle. Keep in mind, though, I'm in charge of assigning chores for the next week. How much do you like cleaning bathrooms?"

"Sorry," came Lexi's response, the giggle still there.

"It's a sad state of affairs when a man can't get any respect from his own flesh and blood," he complained.

Before the teasing could go any further, Rennie turned into the mall parking lot. "Keep an eye out for a spot. It's gotten so Friday nights you can hardly find a place even this far out."

Luckily, Jesse spotted a car starting to back out just as they passed by the store they were headed for. In short order, Rennie maneuvered the van in and the girls started unloading all of their gear.

"Are we working inside the mall or outside?" Becky asked.

"The mall owners gave us permission only to sell outside the stores. We can cover either or both of the two doors into this store. It's up to you girls, but you'll probably sell more if two of you stay at one door and the other sits by the other entrance with me," Rennie answered.

"We want to be at the same table," Brittany and Becky called.

"Is that okay, Lexi?" Jesse asked, turning to his other niece.

"Yeah, no problem as long as you or Rennie stay with me." She picked up two cases of candy and headed for the other door.

Jesse helped her set up one of the tables and then opened the candy cases for her. When everything was set, Lexi used her best salesperson voice and asked, "Well, sir, have you made your selection or would you like more time to browse?"

Jesse couldn't resist the twinkle in his niece's brown eyes that looked so much like his own. He reached for his wallet and counted out the necessary money.

Business was brisk for the first hour and then slowed down after that. Rennie joined Jesse for a cup of coffee, standing where they could see all three girls.

"I hope the temperature doesn't drop much more," Rennie said as she gratefully accepted the mug of coffee from Jesse. "This down vest might not be much to look at, but it usually keeps me pretty warm."

Jesse had been admiring Rennie's attire since they'd arrived. He liked the casual breezy look she achieved with some bright yellow sweats and the red down vest. Her hair was pulled back from her face in a French braid, emphasizing the delicate bone structure of her face. She may not be outfitted in the most expensive clothes in the world, but he found her flair for casual comfort appealing.

"What?" he teased. "You don't want to go for the pathetic angle?"

"It doesn't work for adults," she replied, eyes twinkling. "To use the angle to the best advantage, it takes a certain degree of cuteness that we're lacking."

"I think you're cute," he asserted, hand over his heart in solemn promise.

"So are you, kind sir, but there's nothing like an eight-year-old with pigtails and a few teeth still missing to sell candy in a hurry."

Jesse smiled, enjoying the teasing banter. More and more he was realizing how much his prior relationships with other women had been lacking. All of the women had been attractive and pleasant company. Try as he might, though, he couldn't imagine enjoying himself with any of them standing outside on a chilly evening watching kids selling candy.

Rennie made it all seem like the most natural thing in the world to be doing, just like she had the other night at the band concert. Jesse knew he could become addicted to sharing the mundane details of family life with a woman like Rennie.

No, take that back. Not a woman *like* Rennie—he needed Rennie herself, no substitutes.

Again Jesse thought to himself how much he wanted to have Rennie to himself for an evening. Just as he was about to ask her if she knew someone who could baby-sit all three of the girls, he spied a familiar face among a group of shoppers.

Rennie had held her coffee mug out to ask Jesse for a refill when she noticed he was staring over her head with a look of horror that he quickly masked. Before she could ask what was wrong, he stepped past her and walked toward a woman who'd just stepped out of the store, carrying a dress shrouded in protective plastic.

The strikingly beautiful woman spoke, one eyebrow arched, clearly conveying great displeasure. "Why, Jesse, whatever are you doing here?"

Jesse planted a quick kiss on the blonde's cheek as Rennie watched, jealousy burning through her with shocking intensity. Evidently it showed because Jesse's acquaintance gave her a knowing look.

"Don't you think you should introduce me to your little friend, Jess? After all, if you're going to break a date with me to spend time with her, I should at least know my replacement's name."

Before Jesse could speak, Vanessa pushed by him and held out a perfectly manicured hand to Rennie. "Hello, I'm Vanessa Gilbert, another friend of Jesse's." Her calculating eyes took in Rennie's appearance in a quick glance. She didn't seem impressed by the competition.

"I'm Rennie Sawyer," Rennie answered. She felt compelled to add, "Actually, we're not really friends. I'm just his niece's Trailblazer leader. We're sharing a time slot to sell candy."

Vanessa turned back to Jesse, who was staring at Rennie like she'd grown a second head. "Am I hearing this right, Jesse?" She gestured toward the three girls and their candy. "This is the 'sales meeting with a major candy distributor' that you broke our date for tonight?"

He nodded, quietly watching the play of emotions across Rennie's face—anger, hurt, embarrassment. "I told you last week, Vanessa, that I was staying with my nieces while my brother and his wife are gone. Part of taking care of them is helping them with their projects." He spoke with exaggerated patience, his words clipped and cold.

Evidently, Vanessa realized she wasn't winning any points with the stern-faced man standing next to her by ignoring the girls. "Oh, these little girls are your nieces that I've heard so much about?" She asked Lexi, "Which one are you?"

"I'm Lexi, that's Brittany," she added, pointing at her sister across the way. Lexi moved to stand closer to Rennie, who instinctively put her arm around the dark-headed girl's shoulder. "Do you want to buy some candy?"

Vanessa made a show of deciding which variety would be the best to purchase. "Here, honey, I'll take this one."

She handed Lexi a five-dollar bill to pay for the candy. When Lexi started to make change, Vanessa said, "No, you keep the money. Consider it my contribution to your troop."

"It's a club, not a troop," Lexi retorted bluntly. "And I don't take tips." She handed the money back.

"Lexi!" Jesse broke in. "There's no need for you to be rude to Ms. Gilbert. Now apologize."

"Sorry," she muttered without meeting Vanessa's gaze.

Before the situation could worsen, Rennie took Lexi by the arm and said, "Come on, Lexi, let's leave your uncle and his friend alone for a few minutes. We'll go check on Becky and your sister."

She helped the girls count their money and their candy to see how well they were doing. The entire time, she was painfully aware of the handsome couple standing a short distance away. Of course, Jesse had a life before this week. After all, he was a healthy male in the prime of his life. It was only natural that he'd have a lady friend, maybe even more than one.

But did the woman in question have to be the epitome of all that Robin, and evidently Jesse, had wanted in a woman? Everything that Rennie was lacking this Vanessa person possessed in spades. Her flawless complexion, silvery blond hair, and sense of style that reeked of success and money was enough to make Rennie sick. To top it all off, no doubt Vanessa had a career that paralleled Jesse's own success.

Rennie had taken an intense dislike to Vanessa instantly for reminding her of her inadequacies as a woman. If she were to be fair about it, it really wasn't Vanessa's fault that she was a perfect counterpoint for Jesse. If Rennie wanted to be honest, she had no right to be jealous of anyone Jesse was dating. After all, she had no claim on the man.

But she didn't want to be fair or honest. She fought the urge to snatch the woman bald for just standing near Jesse, and then she wanted to kick him in the seat of his pants for making her feel this way. Damn the man, she'd had a nice life going. After dealing with the guilt and grief over Robin's death, she'd worked hard to establish a pleasant, normal routine for both Becky and herself. The only strong emotions she'd had were in regard to her daughter.

Now here she was, trying to carry on a normal-sounding conversation with Becky and Jesse's nieces on the outside while inside her emotions were in turmoil. Anger and jealousy were vying for dominance, with fear giving them a run for their money. She forced herself to take a calming breath, reminding herself that it wasn't Jesse's fault that Vanessa had picked this night to go shopping.

No, if he hadn't broken his date with Vanessa, they'd be somewhere having an intimate dinner for two or maybe attending one of those parties for the up-and-coming. Instead, he was with his nieces and a woman wearing sweats and her hair in a braid. Where was a fairy godmother when she needed one? Rennie didn't need a ball gown or glass slippers, but it would be rather nice if someone could turn Vanessa into a pumpkin and Jesse into a rat.

She really had to get away to bring herself under control. "Girls, will you be okay for a few minutes? I'm going into the mall to see if I can find some hot chocolate."

"But, Mom, we have half a Thermos of hot chocolate right here," Becky called after her.

"I want some with an inch of real whipped cream floating on top," Rennie answered over her shoulder as she disappeared into the store.

When Jesse noticed Rennie had deserted the girls, he knew he was in big trouble on a second front. On the first line of battle, Vanessa wasn't buying his story that he was trying to avoid hurting her feelings by deliberately misleading her about his so-called sales meeting and the reason for breaking their date.

"Jesse, I'm sorry. Nieces or not, I can't believe that you would think selling candy, of all things, was more important than a chance to meet the partners at my firm. I've been trying for months to set up a casual introduction for you."

Her normally cool blue eyes looked more like the color of arctic ice right now. "It could be months before we get another chance. Now, if you go ask your little friend when she comes back from wherever she wandered off to, I'm sure she'll understand why you need to leave with me. If we hurry, we'll have time to stop at my place and then yours to get dressed and still be only fashionably late for the cocktail party." Her tone clearly indicated that she would not welcome any dissent on his part.

Jesse didn't have to think about his response. "She is not my 'little friend,' Vanessa." His eyes hardened. "Besides, she's not re-sponsible for the care of my nieces while my brother is gone. I am. If it means standing out here pushing chocolates, that's what I'm going to do. I apologize for not telling you the truth in the first place, but I'm staying here until they're done at eight o'clock. Then I'm going to take the girls home and spend the next week and a half watching them."

He tried to soften his next words. "Vanessa, we've been friends for a long time and I value our friendship. I'm sorry if you don't understand my commitment to the kids, but family means more to me than meeting the partners."

" 'Sorry' doesn't cut it with me, Jesse. And as noble-sounding as your dedication is to your nieces, it's that brunette who you're really worried about or you wouldn't keep watching the door for her to come back." Vanessa shifted her purse and dress to her other hand and stepped back from Jesse. "Next time you call me, don't count on a very friendly reception. Now if you'll excuse me, I have more important places to be."

With that, she marched off without looking back once. Although Jesse felt bad about the seemingly irreparable damage to their friend-ship, it couldn't be helped. Lexi, Brittany, Becky, and especially Rennie deserved better than to be left at the mall while he ran off to another in a long line of boring parties.

He'd come to realize in a very short time that he wanted more out of life than networking with money-hungry power brokers. He wanted it all—a job he enjoyed, a place to live that really was a home, and a family of his own to share it with.

He wanted Rennie.

He rejoined the girls. When the line at the candy table shortened a bit, he casually asked Becky, "Where did your mom go?

Standing up to return to her table, Lexi answered for her. "She went looking for hot chocolate." She shrugged as she passed by. "Sounded weird to me because we still have some in the Thermos."

It was worse than he thought. Jesse was sure in the normal course of events that Rennie would never have left the girls alone like this. Even he knew the club rules clearly stated that if there are more than two girls selling candy, the presence of two supervising adults at all times was mandatory, not optional.

His first instinct was to hunt her down and tell her that things weren't as they seemed. Trouble is, they were. She'd been confronted with the existence of another woman in his life. She had proof he'd lied to Vanessa about what he was doing tonight. If Vanessa didn't buy his excuse for misleading her about why he broke their date, Rennie was sure to think he was ashamed to admit he was helping the kids sell candy.

He was willing to admit he wasn't exactly innocent of all charges. All he wanted was the chance to plead his case by explaining extenuating circumstances. That is, if he could think of any that would stand the light of day. Ruefully, he had to feel sort of lucky that the two women hadn't united to rip the lone male to pieces. He'd already failed to negotiate a truce with Vanessa and he had little hope that he'd be more successful with Rennie.

"Is something wrong, Uncle Jess?" Brittany's voice interrupted his thoughts.

Jesse realized he'd been marching from one door to the other while waiting for Rennie to reappear.

"No, everything's okay," he lied. "I'm just trying to be with you two and Lexi at the same time." Before she could express any doubts about his shaky explanation, he turned and headed back toward Lexi.

When Rennie hadn't appeared after another ten minutes, Jesse wasn't the only one getting worried. Becky left Brittany at the table and walked over to where Jesse was standing, still glaring at the store entry as if willpower alone could drag Rennie back through the door.

"Do you know what's taking Mom so long?" Becky's voice quivered a bit.

Jesse's concern must have communicated itself to the girls because when he glanced at them, they all seemed worried. "I'm sure she just got stuck in a long line and will be back in a few more minutes." His smile must have reassured the small girl, because she headed back to sell more candy. His life was sure getting complicated.

Rennie had run out of excuses to avoid rejoining Jesse and the girls. She knew she shouldn't have panicked. The blond beauty was sure to read it as a victory. Besides, Rennie had an obligation to supervise the girls while they finished their last hour of selling candy.

Just being confronted with such painful reminders of everything that had gone wrong between her and Robin had brought her close to tears. She'd had to get out of Jesse's sight before she humiliated herself by crying. The tears were still not far below the surface, and her hold on her emotions was tenuous at best. Several laps up and down the mall hadn't helped much.

At the last minute she'd at least had the presence of mind to actually buy the hot chocolate. If she'd returned to the girls without it, one of them would say something. Rennie wasn't sure she could come up with a logical excuse.

If her fairy godmother could at least manage to have Vanessa gone before Rennie stepped out of that door looming ahead, she'd settle for that much help. She was going to have a hard enough time facing Jesse and the girls, much less her competition.

Now wait! Since when had she admitted to herself that she was in competition for the favors of the divine Mr. Daniels? Hadn't she told herself time and again how wrong he was for her? He was an attorney, for Pete's sake! Was she becoming self-destructive?

She forced herself to be honest about the evening's events. Jesse had obviously chosen to spend the time with Rennie and the girls, not with Vanessa. He'd risked his relationship, and maybe even his career, to sell candy. That was a point for his side. Of course, he'd lied about his plans to Vanessa—definitely a minus.

He seemed to enjoy himself whenever the four of them were together—another plus. Was it the girls he enjoyed or was some of the pleasure from being with her? No answer, no point.

"May I be of help, ma'am? We do have more of those teddies that those mannequins are wearing on the counter over there if you'd like to examine them."

The sales clerk's voice startled Rennie out of her reverie. She realized she'd been lurking in the lingerie department so long she'd drawn the attention of several of the sales staff. Rennie shook her head no and thanked the clerk.

Here she was, just inside the doors, trying to score a game she had never been very good at. Since it wasn't going to get any easier to face her companions, she strode forward and grabbed the door handle. She sent a silent hope heavenward that no one asked her where she'd been for so long, because she couldn't remember a single item that she'd seen other than the teddies.

And she was in no mood to discuss lingerie with Jesse Daniels.

The first thing she noticed was that Jesse was standing alone, watching the door down the way. He definitely was alone, no Vanessa in sight. Rennie quickly glanced around. All three girls were currently busy helping customers choose their candy and collecting the money. With any luck, they'd sold enough that they could leave before their full time was up. She wasn't sure how much longer she could take Jesse's company tonight. She really needed to get home and spend some time exploring her feelings about the man.

Jesse happened to look back toward Brittany and Becky just in time to see Rennie step out of the door and head for her daughter. She glanced rather guiltily toward him and gave him a tentative smile. He released a breath he hadn't been aware he'd been holding. While she wasn't exactly rushing back to his side, she was not ignoring him entirely.

"Hey, Uncle Jess! I just sold my last pack of candy. Don't even have one left to eat on the way home." Lexi proudly held up her envelope bulging with money. "I sold three cases!"

"Honey, that's great!" Jesse told her with genuine approval. "Let's fold up your table and then join the others. From what I saw a few minutes ago, they ought to be about out of candy, too."

He tried to look casual, stretching his arms over his head to limber up from standing in one spot too long. Actually, he was trying to relieve some of the tension in his neck and shoulders that had built up while he'd waited for Rennie's return.

In short order, he had collapsed the table and flattened the candy cases and carried all of it back out to load in the van. Meanwhile, Lexi carried her chair over to the other door and sat down to help her sister deal with the final customers.

When Jesse rejoined the others, they were trying to decide whether to call it a night. Between Becky and Brittany, there were only a few packages of candy left, in fact, they'd sold completely out of the most popular flavor.

He tried to approach quietly, testing the waters. When Rennie didn't immediately go for his throat, he figured he was safe for the moment. "Tell you what," Jesse said, interrupting their conversation, "I'll buy the last few. You won't believe how popular they'll make me when I go into the office." He gave a wicked grin and added,

"Last time I took in candy, it was like a bunch of sharks going into a feeding frenzy."

"Oh, right, Uncle Jess," Lexi retorted, her disbelief obvious.

Jesse held out his hands, performing a sleight-of-hand maneuver that looked like he could pull off the top of his thumb and then reattach it. "True story, ladies. I reached for the last piece of candy that day and accidentally got in the way of one of the meaner sharks. This poor, mangled appendage was the sad result."

For the first few seconds, Jesse had a sympathetic audience. Then one after the other they caught on to the trick and realized they'd been had. Even Rennie had to smile. Due to popular demand, Jesse knelt between the girls and showed them how it was done. Even Becky proudly showed her mom how well she could "dismantle" her thumb.

Rennie watched as Jesse charmed the girls, including her daughter. She had to admit that he really seemed to enjoy spending time with them. All the same, she felt like her emotions were taking off on a roller-coaster ride over which she had no control.

One minute she found herself being drawn to the warmth of his smile. Then there was the simple pleasure he took in gently teasing the girls, making sure to include Becky on an equal basis with his nieces. The next thing she knew, he was getting lost in a business call, forgetting that she was in the room.

How could she deal with the matter of his lying to Vanessa about his plans for the evening? Was he really just trying to offer the woman an explanation that she'd accept easily? Could he be ashamed to be caught chaperoning his nieces while they sold candy?

She had no basis on which to make an informed decision. Her intellect told her all the things about Jesse that should make her run, not walk, away from him as fast as possible. Her heart, on the other hand, denied the obvious facts, pointing instead to his smile, his gentleness with the girls, his funny grumbling before he had his morning coffee. Things that told her the real man underneath the thin veneer of social politeness was someone very special.

Maybe she just needed some time and space to distance herself from the overwhelming presence of the man to think it all through. After all, she'd thought Robin would be a good husband and father. Ultimately, he'd failed in both categories.

Granted, it took two to make a marriage fall apart most of the time. She knew that she could have been more supportive of him and his goals. Especially at first, he'd at least pretended that all of his ambition was directed to providing his family with the good things in life.

In the end, though, he'd become addicted to the adrenaline rush of making just one more killing in the stock market, one more chance to leave his competition behind, eating his dust. Then he was dead, the rush over, the game lost. No one came out a winner, least of all Robin or his family.

"Mom, can we stop for ice cream again on the way home?" Becky's voice called, interrupting Rennie's reverie.

"No, honey, not tonight. It'll be too close to bedtime by the time we get home." She reached for the chairs and started folding them. "We need to get these things loaded into the van and get in out of this chilly air." She gave her daughter a quick hug, then glanced over at Jesse. "Besides, I think Mr. Daniels here has probably had enough of us and packages of candy for one evening."

Rennie let go of Becky and had started to step off the curb to carry a load out to her car when Jesse grabbed her by the arm.

"Let me carry those for you."

"I can handle it," she insisted, tugging her arm free from his grasp.

"I know you can, but sometimes it's okay to let someone else shoulder part of the load for you. I also want to know if you heard me complaining about how we've spent the evening?"

"No," she answered softly.

"Then don't judge me by your husband's standards. I'm here, not because I have to be, but because I want to be." He stepped in front of her, forcing her to look him in the face. "Now listen carefully. I love my nieces and rarely get as much time as I'd like with them. They have busy lives and it's hard to find a time when they don't have something else they're already doing."

He smiled, his brown eyes warm and inviting. "And I'm here because I'll do anything, including selling candy, to spend more time with you. If you don't like that, I'm sorry, but those are the facts. If you don't want to get involved with me, you'll have to be the one to end it."

He waited, giving her a few seconds to respond. When she

couldn't think of anything to say, he brushed a quick kiss across her lips and stepped back out of her way.

Lightening the mood, he motioned her in front of him. "Lead on, MacDuff! Show me where to stow this and let's get these tired old bones home to bed."

Rennie led the way to the van, her lips still savoring his kiss, her traitorous heart wishing for more.

Seven

"Hey, Uncle Jess!" Lexi called down the staircase. "I'm done with my room."

Jesse stepped out of the kitchen and looked up the stairs at his niece. He glanced at his watch. "By my calculations, you just set the new world record for bedroom cleaning."

"I vacuumed and everything," she claimed.

"Everything?" he asked with a great deal of skepticism. Jesse considered the matter. "Let me ask you this. Did you clean to my standards or your mom's?"

"I don't understand what you mean."

"Well, for example, when I vacuum, I just do the parts that show. Your mom actually sweeps under things like beds and tables." His brown eyes twinkled as he watched Lexi think it over. "So whose standards did you meet?"

"Yours, definitely," she finally decided. "Is that okay?"

"Well, since your mom won't be back for another week, we'll let it slide. Just keep in mind that we'll have to bring the whole house up to snuff before next Sunday when your folks get home."

The telephone rang just as Jesse headed back for the kitchen.

Before he could reach the wall phone, he heard Brittany yell down, "I'll get it!" and the sound of her feet pounding down the hall upstairs. He waited briefly to see if the call was for him. When he didn't hear anything, he returned to his chores in the kitchen.

He was doing several things at once. The washer and dryer were both running, and he was working on the ironing for the week. Sometimes he sent his shirts to the cleaners, but he really preferred to do them himself. Since he wasn't working in the office, he'd been wearing more casual clothes and thought it a good time to get ahead on his ironing. Besides, it seemed like everything the girls owned was cotton and had to be at least touched up. He'd never imagined himself pressing ruffles and flounced hems.

After one particularly trying dress, he muttered to himself, "With all this experience, I'll make some lucky person a wonderful wife."

"What'd you say?" Brittany asked.

Jesse jumped, not having heard her come into the room. In the process he burned his finger with the iron. "Damn, that hurt!" Sucking on the wounded appendage, he apologized, "Sorry about that. I should have said, 'Darn, that hurt.' "

"That's okay," Brittany answered, pushing her glasses back up her nose into position. "Mom always runs cold water on a burn like that. Seems to help."

Knowing she'd wait till he complied with her eight-year-old wisdom, he set down the iron and dutifully held his finger under running water. "You're right, it does feel better." After shutting the water off, he asked, "Did you need something, pumpkin?"

"Oh, yeah, that's why I came down. That was Grandma on the phone."

Surprised, Jesse interrupted her, "When did she get back from her lake home? I thought she was staying there for another week or two?"

"She was," Brittany answered. "But the friend she went with got called home for some reason. Grandma said they were planning on going back to the lake on Monday."

Jesse resumed his ironing, carefully keeping his fingers out of the way this time. "Was she calling to check in or did she want something else?"

"She wanted to know if Lexi and I could come spend the night with her. She wants us to go to church with her tomorrow and then out for brunch. She'd have us home after dinner tomorrow night." Brittany grinned as she added, "Grandma said she thought you might like a break by now."

"Do you want to go?"

"Sure, it's okay with me."

"Did you ask your sister?"

"She's already packing. I thought we ought to ask you first and then pack."

"Well, thanks a lot for that," Jesse answered dryly. "It's fine with me, though I'll miss you both. Do you need any help getting ready?"

"No. We go pretty often, so packing is a cinch."

As she ran out of the room, he called after her, "Tell your grandmother that I'll bring you over in about an hour. I want to finish the rest of this ironing before we go."

Just after lunchtime Jesse found himself driving back to the house all alone. Although he was free to go to his condo until tomorrow night when the girls would get home, he didn't relish the thought of either the packing or the drive. He mentally ran through his options.

He didn't feel like working outside particularly, even though the lawn really should be mowed soon. He'd never lived in Mukilteo long enough to develop any friendships, so he couldn't just drop in on any of the neighbors in hopes they were in the mood for company. Or could he?

Without giving it further thought, he turned toward Rennie's house rather than returning home. With any luck, she'd be willing to offer him a cup of coffee. Besides, he was curious to see how she would react to him after everything that had happened at the mall.

He almost drove past her house without recognizing it. If he hadn't caught a quick glimpse of Becky, he would have missed it altogether. The front of the house was all but obscured by a huge pile of the ornamental bark commonly used in the Northwest to fill in flower beds and around bushes and trees. Rennie must have had ten cubic yards of it piled in her driveway.

He pulled to the curb and backed up to park on the street in front of Rennie's house. As he got out of the car, Becky came running across the lawn.

"Did you bring Brittany with you, Mr. Daniels?"

"Sorry, Becky, it's just me this time. Brittany and Lexi went over to spend the night with their grandmother."

"Hey, that's what I'm doing, too!"

Jesse pretended to misunderstand. "You're going to spend the weekend with Brittany's grandma?"

Becky giggled. "No, with my Grandma Sawyer. She's coming to pick me up soon." Then Becky turned serious. "Mom says it's best for me to go because all this bark is going to make her very crabby before she gets it spread out."

Before Jesse could respond, a feminine voice broke in. "Hey, squirt! Do you have to announce to the whole world that I'm a real witch today?"

Rennie was standing near the garage. She wore an oversized T-shirt knotted at her waist and faded jeans with holes in the knees. A few strands of hair had pulled out of her ponytail, giving evidence that she'd already been hard at work.

"Sorry, Mom."

"That's okay, sweetheart. If Mr. Daniels is afraid of witches, maybe it's better he know that there's one around. You run on now and finish packing your bag. Grandma will be here soon."

Just before Becky disappeared inside the house, Rennie called after her, "And don't forget your toothbrush this time!"

After Becky was gone, Jesse glanced at the tool in Rennie's hand and asked, "Since when did witches start wearing jeans and riding shovels instead of brooms?" He pointedly made a slow survey of her long legs.

She arched an eyebrow and gave him a very superior look. "For your information, witches have known for centuries that shovels work much better than brooms when it comes to landscaping yards. Maybe attorneys weren't smart enough to catch on as quickly."

He laughed, revealing a small dimple that Rennie hadn't seen before. She had noticed, though, how well his shoulders filled out the short-sleeved knit shirt he had on.

"That's one possible interpretation of the facts, Madam Witch, but perhaps the truth of the matter is that attorneys have usually been able to afford to hire someone else to use shovels for them. Witches, on the other hand, usually have had other fates in store for them." He spoke in his most officious voice.

"Yeah, and that really burns me up!" she quipped.

He groaned. "Don't tell me you like puns."

"All right, I won't *spell* it out for you, but don't say you weren't warned." She snickered at his pained look. "Now, if you want to continue this conversation, you'll have to talk while I shovel or I'll never get this stuff hauled out back." She walked over to the pile of bark and started loading up a wheelbarrow she had parked next to the heap.

"I can't stand by and watch you do all the work without feeling guilty," Jesse told her after watching just a minute or so.

"You could always help, I guess," she replied without interrupting her rhythm.

"I could also just shut my eyes," he answered, then playfully leered and added, "but then I couldn't see the wonderful things those jeans do to your legs."

She stood up straight and glared at him. "Hold it there, buster. I'm looking hours of back-breaking labor in the face and I don't need comments from the peanut gallery to distract me."

"Do I?" he asked, with a not-quite-innocent smile on his face.

"Do you what?" she asked, confused.

"Distract you?"

She shook her head in exasperation. "I'm not going to add to your already inflated ego." She brushed a strand of hair back out of her face. "What are you doing here, anyway? After last night, I would have thought you'd be burning up the phone lines trying to make peace with Buffie."

"You mean Vanessa?" Jesse asked innocently. He was really enjoying the possibility that Rennie was jealous.

"Vanessa, Buffie, whatever. All those yuppie names sound the same after a while." She put a little too much body language into her next shovel load and overshot the wheelbarrow. She muttered something short and succinct under her breath.

Jesse coughed to cover a laugh. "No, I didn't call Vanessa last night or today. I explained to her why I was with you and the girls. If she couldn't accept that, I'm not going to plead with her. Besides, Van and I go out only to business-related functions. I think she'd faint if I asked her over just for an evening of pleasure."

When Rennie didn't respond, he asked. "How about you? Would you faint if I asked you out for an evening of pleasure tonight?"

That stopped her. She stuck the shovel into the bark and turned to face him. "Just what do you mean by 'an evening of pleasure'?"

"You know, dinner, dancing, that sort of thing." His brown eyes sparkled with devilment. "Why, Rennie Sawyer! What did you think I meant? I'm not easy, you know."

"No."

"No, you won't go out with me?"

"No, I mean I wouldn't faint if you asked me out for an evening of pleasure." She returned to her shoveling. "I might refuse, but I won't faint."

"Why would you refuse?" he asked, putting his hand on the shovel to prevent her from ignoring him while she worked.

"Well, for one thing, I don't have a baby-sitter."

"That won't wash, lady. I happen to know your daughter is going to spend the night with her grandmother."

"But you don't have a baby-sitter," she said, sounding hopeful.

"No, but I don't have my nieces, either," he answered triumphantly. "I just dropped them off at their grandmother's."

"I've got bark to spread." She knew her arguments were growing weaker. The bark would still be there tomorrow. If she kept pushing him away, Jesse might not be.

"I'll help. You spread. I'll load the wheelbarrow and deliver the stuff wherever you want it."

"We'll both be tired." She paused to stretch her back as if to emphasize how weary she was getting already.

"We can go to bed early." He jumped back when she started after him with the shovel. "Hey, I just meant we can make an early night of it, if that's what you want. I just thought you'd like to eat out after doing all this work."

Rennie brushed back her hair from her face, using the time to look at Jesse thoughtfully. Finally, she said, "All right, I give up. We'll shovel bark as long as we can stand it, and then we can grab a quick bite somewhere."

Knowing victory was his, Jesse took the spade from her hand and started shoveling the bark with a vengeance. Rennie left him to his labors to check on Becky's progress getting her suitcase ready.

A few minutes later, Rennie stepped off the front porch with two glasses of fresh lemonade in her hands. Jesse had gotten a Walkman out of his car. He was wearing earphones and singing along to music no one else could hear. While he was unaware of her scrutiny, she took advantage of the moment to enjoy just watching him.

The knit shirt clung lovingly to the well-defined muscles in his shoulders. The effect each rippling motion had on her libido was frightening. And those snug jeans of his ought to be outlawed around unsuspecting females of all ages.

"My dear, are you getting so desperate that you've had to stoop to drooling over the hired help?"

Rennie jumped, almost dropping the lemonade. She whirled around to find herself face-to-face with her mother-in-law.

"Madeline! You startled me—I didn't hear you drive up." Rennie hoped she didn't look as guilty as she felt. Imagine, getting caught ogling a man at her age.

Her mother-in-law, still lovely well into her sixties, was looking past Rennie at Jesse when she answered. "I had to park down the street since the driveway was full of bark. By the way, if that BMW in front of the house belongs to that man, I wonder if you can afford his services."

"Not to worry, ma'am, I let Rennie have my services in exchange for hers." Jesse stuck the shovel into the bark and left it standing there while he walked over to join the women in the shade by the porch. Evidently he'd turned the radio off when neither woman was watching him.

He paused before continuing, enjoying Rennie's discomfiture. "Actually, she's helping me out with her vast experience in Trail-blazer candy sales, so I'm paying her back—her brains for my muscles." He didn't miss Rennie's quick glance at his shoulders, but he hid his pleasure that she obviously liked what she saw.

The silver-haired lady standing next to Rennie held out her hand and introduced herself. "I'm Madeline Sawyer, Rennie's mother-in-law."

"Jesse Daniels," he answered, shaking her hand. "You may know my nieces, Lexi and Brittany Daniels."

"Sure, they're great kids. I've even had Brittany come spend the night with Becky at my place a couple of times. Are they in the house with her?"

"No, they went to their grandmother's for the night."

"Rennie, are you going to hold on to that lemonade till it gets warm?" Madeline asked. "If not, I'm sure Mr. Daniels would appreciate a glass and I know I would. Why don't you give those two to us and go get yourself a fresh one? While you're inside, see if Becky is about ready."

Rennie wasn't sure she liked the gleam in Madeline's eyes. But short of being rude, she had no choice but to relinquish the glasses and leave Jesse alone with her matchmaking mother-in-law.

As soon as Rennie was out of sight, Madeline asked, "So, Mr. Daniels—"

"Please, make it Jesse," he interrupted.

She nodded. "Jesse, then. How long have you known my daughter-in-law?"

"About a week now." Before she could ask any more questions, he continued with a smile, "I'm thirty-two, single, no real bad habits, and have a steady job."

Madeline had the good grace to be embarrassed. "I'm sorry, but this is the first time I've seen Rennie let a man close enough to be on a first-name basis who wasn't at least my age or married. It's hard not to be pretty excited about it."

"I'm pretty excited about it myself," Jesse replied, pausing briefly to take a long drink from his glass. "Of course, there is the problem of my occupation."

"Oh, no, don't tell me you're a stockbroker?" The distress in her voice was obvious.

"Worse—I'm an attorney."

"Well, that is tragic, but I'm willing to overlook it if Rennie is. I wouldn't want her hurt, you understand." Her words were softly spoken, but the steel underneath was very real.

"I don't plan to, but it's hard even to get her to agree to a pizza unless we have the girls as chaperones."

"Yes, that sounds like Rennie." She gave Jesse a stern look. "I loved my son very much, but I'm not blind to what he did to Rennie and my granddaughter. Some men are just never cut out to be husbands, much less fathers." She sighed and shook her head, lost in her memories.

With that she followed Rennie into the house, unaware of the devastating effect her words had on the man she left standing outside.

Jesse returned to his work, woodenly pushing the wheelbarrow around the end of the garage toward the backyard. Yes, some men were not marriage material, and he was fully aware that he was one of them.

A few minutes later, Rennie came looking for Jesse. She found him standing in the deep shade, staring off into the trees behind her house. The set of his shoulders told her that something was wrong. He wasn't just taking a break from the shoveling.

She approached carefully, unsure of her welcome. "Jesse?" she called softly, not wanting to startle him out of his reverie. "Is something wrong?"

He didn't move, and at first she wasn't sure that he'd heard her. Then he took a deep breath and straightened his shoulders, as if to prepare himself to face her.

"No, everything is fine."

He didn't sound fine, though. Rennie found herself wanting to put her arms around him to offer comfort for whatever was causing him such pain.

"Did my mother-in-law say something to upset you? She means well, but sometimes she can ride roughshod over folks."

Jesse must have realized that he was worrying Rennie. "No, she's a very nice woman. She has good taste, too, because she thinks a lot of you. She even restrained herself from asking what my intentions were."

"Well, that was noble of her—I'm sure she was dying to, you know." Rennie looped her arm through Jesse's and tugged him out of the coolness of the shade and into the warmth of the sun. "Come on, lawyer man, I'm not gonna let you shirk your duties as chief shoveler around here. If you want me to pay half on dinner tonight, you'll have to put in a decent day's work." Seeing the grim look on his face start to relax, she teased, "Of course, as an attorney, you probably never have to do any hard work."

He had to laugh at her outrageous statement. "Hey, now, I've worked hard. Why sometimes I have to sharpen my own pencils and"—he paused for effect—"once I even got a file out of the cabinet without my secretary's help."

"Well, all I can say is that I'm glad we have a shovel handy, because it's starting to get pretty deep around here." She snickered and tried to dodge him as he grabbed for her.

He caught her by the ponytail and hauled her back into his arms. She went willingly after only token resistance, putting her hands first on his shoulders, then tangling them in his hair at the base of his neck. When his lips found hers, she was the one who deepened the kiss. She felt the desperation in his embrace and wondered at it.

All she could do was offer the comfort of a kiss and hope that it was enough.

"Well, how do we decide who gets that final piece of pizza?" Jesse asked after he polished off the last slice on his plate.

"I guess I should be polite and offer to let you have it," Rennie answered. "After all, you did browbeat me into letting you pay for dinner."

"Great!" Jesse said as he reached for the sole occupant of a deep-dish pizza pan.

Before he could get it, however, Rennie grabbed the pan and held it out of his reach. "Just a minute there, buster. I said I should be polite. I never said I would be."

"Aw, come on, Rennie, I'm a growing boy and need all the nourishment I can get." The twinkle in his eyes belied the innocent expression on his face.

Rennie snorted. "The best deal I'll offer you is to split the piece right down the middle and I get the half with the most mushrooms on it."

He appeared to give the matter some thought. "Well, I guess that would be best, but only if I'm the one who cuts the slice."

Rennie relinquished the pan after a momentary hesitation. She leaned forward, resting her elbows on the table, and watched closely as Jesse meticulously measured and cut the remaining piece into two equal halves.

"There. Are you satisfied?" he asked.

"Yep, you did a fine job."

She waited till Jesse took his share, then picked up her fork and reached for hers. Just before she could, Jesse took the knife, sliced the tip off her slice, and popped it in his mouth.

"You rat, that was my piece!" Rennie complained indignantly. "Now give me the other one."

"No way, lady. You contracted with me to cut the slice, which I did. As your attorney of record in this matter, I'm entitled to my fee plus expenses." His smile had a definite smugness about it.

"How do you figure?"

"Well, this piece," he said, pointing at the one on his plate, "is my fee. That part off of yours covers the energy expended in handling all the details of this transaction. Hence, I was entitled to a bite of yours."

Laughing, Rennie gave up and took what was left of her piece and ate it with relish. "You nut, I never know when to take you seriously."

"Well, how about now? I'd like to spend tomorrow with you.

What do you think?" He picked up his soft drink and sipped through the straw, looking at Rennie over the rim of the glass while he waited for her decision.

Rennie had watched Jesse gradually shake off the strange mood he'd been in after Madeline left with Becky. Since they'd reached the restaurant, he'd appeared relaxed and seemed to be enjoying himself. The thought of having him to herself without the girls was tempting.

"Sure, why not? What did you have in mind?"

"Well, I thought maybe a ferry ride up to the San Juan Islands might be just the ticket. If the weather is nice like it was today, the ride should be beautiful. If it's rainy, we can still relax and enjoy the ride inside the ferry."

Rennie knew the trip through the islands would indeed be lovely, but for her the real appeal was having Jesse to herself for an entire day.

"Sounds fine to me," she said. "What time do you think we'll get back?"

"We should be able to make the round trip and still be home by about six. Is that early enough?"

"I don't think it will be a problem. I'll call my mother-in-law when I get home tonight and check with her. As long as it doesn't mess up any plans she has for tomorrow evening, six should be fine."

Jesse looked pleased at her easy acceptance of his offer. "Speaking of getting home tonight, I guess we'd better be headed that way. I don't know about you, but every bone in my body is reminding me of all the bark we shoveled today."

He stretched his arms out to the side and rolled his shoulders to loosen up. "Please tell me that marathon yard work is not a favorite hobby of yours. My poor old body couldn't handle it, I'm afraid."

"Nope, I only indulge myself with a bark-a-thon about once every two or three years. You just happened to hit it lucky today." Of course, if Jesse's "old body" looked any better to her, Rennie wasn't sure if she could stop herself from leaping over the table and attacking him.

He groaned as he stood up. "If that's luck, I'd hate to see what happens to me when things aren't going my way." After he threw some bills on the table for a tip, he offered his hand to Rennie and helped her up from the seat.

"Come on, lady. If we hurry, I just might be able to stay awake long enough to get us both home safely."

Once outside, they started walking to where Jesse had parked his car.

"I still can't believe that you drove around the block four times just to find a parking spot. I'd have used the lot next to the restaurant if it had been my van," Rennie complained good-naturedly as they headed up a particularly steep hill.

"I know it's almost an obsession, but I just can't deal with other people parking too close to my car." Jesse managed to look both sheepish and defensive at the same time.

Rennie was uncomfortably aware of how much Jesse's car reminded her of all the superficial things Robin had held near and dear to his heart. "Yeah, well, I suppose a damaged BMW does cost you a lot of points in the game."

Confused, Jesse asked, "What game?"

"Well, I've always called it the 'Lifestyles of the Rich and Yuppie.' " Belatedly, she realized how insulting her words must have sounded to Jesse.

"Go on." Yes, there was a definite coolness underlying his tone.

"Well, after a while, I started keeping track of all the things that Robin felt were important in creating the image of a rising young executive." The darkness obscured Jesse's face, so she couldn't tell how he was reacting to her words. What had started as a joke was threatening the easy camaraderie they had enjoyed all evening.

"What kind of things?" His words were short and clipped.

"I'm sorry," Rennie answered. "I didn't mean to make a big deal of this."

"No big deal, Rennie. I just want to know what you meant."

She hesitated, glancing nervously at Jesse, and then finally answered him. "When Robin got to where things mattered more than we did, I sort of assigned point value to all the trappings of success and kept score. Name-brand clothes were ten points, the right restaurants were fifteen, espresso makers five. When he'd drag me to cocktail parties where I didn't know anyone, I amused myself by keeping score."

They walked in silence the rest of the way to the car. When they were both buckled in, Jesse pulled away from the curb and headed east toward the interstate. Rennie was frantically trying to think of a new topic of conversation when Jesse spoke up.

"Just what is the point value of a late-model BMW?"

The curious monotone in which the words were spoken did more to chill Rennie than the cool spring breeze outside had.

"It was an automatic win."

"Well, I guess it's nice to know that I'm a winner in someone's opinion," Jesse finally said, a weariness in his voice that hadn't been there earlier.

Eight

Rennie wished she'd never started this discussion. Now that she had, she didn't know how to get out of it. Maybe she should try to apologize again.

"I didn't mean to insult you, you know," she whispered, hoping he'd understand how really sorry she was.

"That's okay. Don't worry about it." Jesse took a deep breath and asked, "Are we still on for tomorrow?"

"If you still want to go, I'd love to. A day on the Sound would be heavenly." Rennie sat quietly and wailed for Jesse to answer.

"I'll pick you up about seven in the morning if you can be ready that early. If we want to have time to browse in Friday Harbor, we should catch one of the first ferries out."

"Sounds fine," Rennie answered. She wished she could see Jesse's face to better gauge his mood, but at least his voice sounded friendlier again. Maybe he'd accepted her apology.

In no time at all, Jesse was turning the car into Rennie's driveway. When she started to get out of the car, he stopped her.

"Wait, let me play the gentleman." He got out and walked around to her side of the car and opened the door with a flourish. "Madam, shall I escort you inside or leave you safely at the door?" He offered her his hand to help her out of the car.

Briefly, she wondered what he had in mind if she invited him in, but she decided she really shouldn't. Reluctant to let go, however, she entwined her fingers in the warm strength of his hand as they walked toward the porch. "I'd offer you some coffee, but all I have is the real stuff with caffeine and everything. If we want to get an early start, I guess we should go right to bed."

She heard his muffled choke and groaned. "I didn't mean we

should, well, you know," she said. "What I meant to say is that after tonight we'd need our rest."

By then he was laughing at her embarrassment, the easy humor of the early evening back in full force. "I hate to say it, but you're right. We really do need to get some"—he paused for effect—"sleep, that is."

She punched him in the arm. "You rat! One little slip of the tongue, and you'll probably never let me forget it."

"You could try to bribe me." He pulled her into his arms, nuzzling her hair, breathing deeply of the fresh scent that was uniquely hers.

"What would it cost me?" Her arms went around his waist as she leaned back slightly to look him in the face.

"Well, for starters you could let me have my wicked, wicked way with you for the next few minutes."

"How few?" The coolness of the evening was giving way to the heat of Jesse's embrace.

"I figure I could last about six minutes without totally losing it." He pressed a series of soft kisses from her temple down to her neck.

She arched her neck to the side, giving him easier access. "Losing what?" She was having difficulty concentrating on the conversation.

"Losing all sense of our surroundings," he murmured in her ear as he gently nipped her lobe. "You might note that we're standing on your front porch with the lights on. Much more time than that, and your neighbors will get an interesting eyeful, I'm afraid."

When his lips finally found hers, Rennie was sorely tempted to throw caution to the wind and let the neighbors be shocked, or better yet, to let Jesse in the front door. It was Jesse who finally pulled back from the edge of the passion that threatened to engulf them.

"I'd better be going, Rennie." His soft words made her name a caress. "I'll see you in the morning, bright and early."

Rennie laughed. When she spoke, her voice was huskier than normal. "Jesse Daniels, remember that I've seen you in the morning. You may be here early, but I'm willing to bet that you won't be bright until you've had several cups of coffee. In fact, maybe I should drive?"

He tried to act insulted, but in the end he just grinned. "No, I'll drive. Just don't expect me to talk coherently until I'm on my third cup." He planted a quick kiss on her lips and stood back while she unlocked her front door and went inside.

She waved one last time from her front window as he backed out of the driveway. Rennie sighed and turned away as he drove out of sight. She hoped a good night's sleep would help her sort out her complex feelings about Jesse Daniels.

The morning dawned gray and cloudy. Rennie listened for the weather forecast on the radio before deciding what to wear. After hearing the prediction of cool temperatures and intermittent rain, she settled on comfortable jeans and a blouse with a sweatshirt over it. After pulling her nylon jacket out of the hall closet, she was as ready as anyone could be for the unpredictable weather of the Northwest.

At seven o'clock sharp, she heard a knock at the door. She opened it to find Jesse standing there doing his best to look cheerful and alert. Without saying a word, she motioned him into the foyer, placing a large mug of hot coffee into his hand.

"Bless you, woman," he said after he took the first drink. "This is cup number two. With any luck, I'll be functioning at almost full capacity before we reach the ferry." Although his clothes were neat and his hair combed, he still looked like someone who'd just unwillingly crawled out of bed.

Rennie shook her head and smiled. "You wait here while I grab my purse and check the back door. Then I'll lead you out to the car. Wouldn't want to leave a man in your condition wandering aimlessly around the neighborhood."

As she walked away, she thought she heard him mutter something derogatory about smart-mouthed morning people. In short order, they were in Jesse's car and on the highway headed north up the coast toward the town of Anacortes.

An hour later, they reached the ferry terminal and Jesse bought their tickets. Since the big green-and-white car ferry was due to leave in less than fifteen minutes, they hurried on board. Naturally, the first place Jesse headed was the canteen to get his beloved third cup of caffeine.

Rennie waited awhile for Jesse's coffee to take effect before trying to start a conversation. When she heard the ferry horn blow and felt the boat start to move, she decided the caffeine had had enough time to start working.

"Do you spend much time out on the water?"

"No," he answered. "In fact, it's been years since I've been on one of these. When I was in college and needed to get away from town for the day, I'd splurge and buy a ticket. I'd take my textbooks with me and ride back and forth across the Sound while I studied. It was a cheap form of entertainment."

The picture he painted of a young student riding the ferries alone was hard to reconcile to the image of the successful attorney sitting next to her. Whenever Rennie felt like she had him figured out, he'd reveal a new facet of his life or personality that left her more confused than before.

Today he had on a designer sweater and jeans that must have cost a pretty penny. His shoes were well worn, but the brand name on them didn't come cheap. While she had to admit that he looked great in anything, he wore expensive clothes with the unconscious grace of those born with money. It was hard to picture him having to worry about the cost of a simple ferry ticket.

"I remember those poor student days myself," she said when he quit talking.

"Yeah, what's your very worst horror story?" he asked. As he spoke, his brown eyes seemed to dare her to top whatever memory he was thinking about.

"Well, Robin and I married my freshman year. There was one week that all we had to eat for four days was cold cereal and milk. When we couldn't face another bowl of the stuff, we went uptown to one of the commercial blood banks and sold our blood for food money."

"Is that the best you can do?" he scoffed.

"I suppose you can top that?"

"Well, I have to admit I got pretty tired of living on boxed cereal and macaroni and cheese at times, too," he admitted. "The worst thing, though, was being a live model for the art department one quarter."

Rennie couldn't believe her ears. She quickly suppressed the wish that she'd been among the students in that class. "You mean you stood there without any . . . I mean, well, you know. In front of an entire art class?"

"Yeah, I did." He walked over to the door of the canteen with her and led her outside. The sun had broken through the clouds temporarily.

Jesse put on his sunglasses so Rennie wasn't able to read the expression in his eyes. His dimples were showing, though, so she guessed the memories weren't too painful for him.

"Any chance that someday I might see you in all your, um, glory in a local art museum?"

"Heaven forbid!" he exclaimed, sounding horrified by the prospect. "Besides, it was a modern art class. Even if you did see one of their pictures, I might have three eyes, four arms, and an extra, um, appendage or two." He leered playfully at her over the top of his glasses.

"How did your parents feel about their hardworking son posing in the nude?" She instantly regretted the question because Jesse's dimples died as soon as she asked it.

"Sorry, bad question, I guess."

He reached over and casually put his arm around her shoulders, pulling her closer. "No, it's okay. But in answer to your question, they didn't know. My dad died in a car wreck when Mark and I were little. And we lost Mom when I was fifteen."

"Oh, Jess, I'm sorry. I know from experience that it's hard for kids when one parent dies, much less both. What did your mother die of?"

His words were bleak. "I didn't say that she died. I said we lost her. Or more accurately, she lost us. I was being such a brat at school, one weekend she left me with Mark to see if he could do anything with me. While I was there, she moved and left no forwarding address. Evidently, she didn't take ours with her either, because we've never heard another word from her."

Stricken with sorrow for the boy Jesse had been, Rennie fought back the tears burning in her eyes. His tone of voice and demeanor told her that her sympathy would not be welcome.

"I don't know how a mother could abandon her kids like that."

"Well, looking back, I'd say that she'd always been pretty dependent on my dad for everything. Without him to make all her decisions for her, she probably had a hard time coping with life."

"That doesn't excuse what she did," Rennie said. Her anger at the damage done by the woman years ago rang clearly in every word.

"No, I guess not. I mean, I don't know how any mother could

leave a son like Mark behind." The quietness of his voice did little to mask the hurt behind the words.

Before she could ask why he felt that Mark was more worthy of a mother's loyalty than he himself was, he took her by the arm and headed toward the bow end of the deck.

"Let's enjoy the sunshine while we can," he explained.

She accepted his decision to end the conversation and avoid the painful memories of his youth. Besides, the wind coming off the bow was too strong to make for easy conversation. Jesse leaned back against the railing facing the Cascade Mountains rising above green-cloaked foothills to the east. Rennie looped her arm through his as they lost themselves in private thoughts.

The afternoon passed gently, with the sounds of seagulls and the tangy smell of the saltwater in the air. They spent hours pouring over the various souvenirs in the shops in Friday Harbor, trying to decide which ones were tacky enough to please Rennie's daughter and Jesse's nieces.

After the first couple of shops, it became a contest to see which one could unearth the most outlandish selection. They finally settled on three neon-colored visor caps with geoduck clams wishing them greetings from San Juan Island. Hand in hand, they wandered back down to the docks and had clam chowder, broiled salmon fillets, and fresh-baked bread for lunch.

As they lingered over dessert and coffee until the ferry was due back, Rennie said, "This was a great way to spend the day, Jesse. It's so easy to get caught up in the routine stuff and forget how beautiful the Sound is, not to mention the islands. I can't remember a day when I've felt so relaxed. Thank you." She smiled into Jesse's eyes across the table.

"You're welcome. By the way, did you notice that the sunshine I ordered held out for the entire trip?" He leaned back in his chair, stretching his long legs out in front of him.

Rennie's eyes drifted down the length of his legs and back up. She blinked, shifting her gaze to his face and hoping her expression didn't reveal the effect all that taut denim was having on her.

"Want to head for the dock and enjoy the last of that sunshine?" she asked.

"Sure, might as well get my money's worth out of it. You know, the weathermen were all set for another gray day. I'd hate to tell you how much it cost to get them to change the forecast just for us."

She laughed and followed him out of the restaurant.

The rain held off until they were in a long line of traffic heading south down the highway toward Seattle. Evidently, everyone who'd escaped the city for the weekend or just for the day had picked the same time to go home. Cars were running at the speed limit when huge raindrops started hitting the windshield with a resounding splash.

Jesse reached down and turned the wipers on high speed and raised the temperature on the heater and defrosters. Once the sun had disappeared behind the darkening clouds, it had gotten increasingly colder.

Not wanting to distract him in such adverse driving conditions, Rennie sat quietly and stared out of the window, watching the scenery passing in a gray haze. Jesse cursed and swerved as a car suddenly changed lanes in front of him without signaling.

"Damn, I wish this rain could have waited another hour. All it will take is somebody hitting his brakes too hard and we'll have chaos." They were the first words Jesse had said since the weather had worsened.

He glanced over apologetically. "Sorry, I know I'm not being the best company right now. I swear, Seattle drivers never seem to know how to drive in the rain. As hard as this stuff is coming down, it's liable to get worse before it gets better."

"Well, I'm in no particular hurry if you want to stop somewhere for coffee and wait it out a bit," Rennie said. "Of course," she added after glancing at the sky, "there's no guarantee that the rain is going to let up anytime soon."

"No, I think we'd better just keep going. Traffic is bound to be heavier later. Anyway, I promised Vickie's mom I'd pick up the girls before eight o'clock. At the rate we're moving, we'll be cutting it pretty close as it is."

Rennie was growing more concerned about Jesse. The tension radiating from him was almost palpable. He was gripping the steering wheel so tightly that his knuckles were almost white.

"Would some music help?" Her voice was soft with concern.

"What?" He glanced quickly at Rennie, then returned his gaze to the road ahead.

"I said, would some quiet music help relax you? You seem pretty tense."

He took a deep breath, apparently trying to ease up a bit. "Sure, something soft and easy would be nice. I don't mean to be so uptight. I just don't want anything to happen."

"Do you have any tapes in the car, or should I try for some easy-listening music on the radio?"

"The tapes are in the glove compartment. I'm not sure what you'll find, though. Brittany and Lexi had some of their stuff in there the other day." He shuddered.

Rennie opened the glove compartment and inspected the possibilities. She held up her first choice. "How do you feel about rap?"

He frowned without looking away from the road. "Try again, please."

"Well, would you prefer heavy metal?" she teased.

He rolled his eyes as he pleaded, "Have some pity on me, woman!"

She relented. "I guess we'll just have to make do with this one by Whitney Houston."

"You rat, you were holding out on me, weren't you?"

At least he was smiling a bit. For a while there, she'd feared his face would take on a permanent frown.

Soon the notes of one of her favorite ballads filled the car. After the second song started, Rennie could see a noticeable difference in Jesse. While he was still intent on his driving, he was softly humming along with the music and sitting easier in the seat.

The warmth of the car and the gentle sound of the songs soon lulled Rennie into a pleasant state of drowsiness. When she started to nod off, she shook her head to clear the cobwebs and sat up straighter.

"Why don't you go on and sleep, Ren? You've had a hectic couple of days."

She couldn't quite stifle a yawn. "Sorry about that—it's not the company. Long car rides always do this to me. Will you be okay if I do? If you need my company to keep you awake, say so. After all, your weekend has been as busy as mine."

"No, go ahead. Besides, Whitney and I want to be alone for a while."

"In your dreams, Daniels," she retorted as she snuggled into the comfort of the leather upholstery.

She was almost asleep when she felt him awkwardly tuck his jacket around her with one hand. It smelled of Jesse; she inhaled deeply and sank deeper into sleep.

She was never sure if she really heard Jesse or if she just dreamed him saying, "Rest well, my dream lady."

Unaware of how much time passed while she slept, Rennie was jerked awake by the sound of brakes screaming for a hold on wet pavement. Her eyes flew open to the sight of Jesse struggling to control the BMW as he guided it to a stop on the shoulder of the road.

"What happened? Are you okay?" Her voice came out high-pitched with fright.

Without answering her, Jesse hit the steering wheel with his fist, swearing viciously. He jerked the car door open and got out, his voice shaking with barely contained fury. "Damn, I knew something like this would happen. All I can say is if that idiot damaged this car, I swear I'll rip his heart out!" Then, slamming the door behind him, he disappeared into the rainy night.

Stunned by Jesse's outburst, Rennie remained motionless for several seconds, waiting for her sleep-clouded mind to clear. Gradually, she became aware of the pinging of the rain on the metal roof of the car. She could also discern the outline of another car parked in front of Jesse's on the shoulder.

Although the rain and gathering darkness blurred much of the detail, the car ahead looked like a full-sized older model. Two figures huddled beside it were outlined in the glare of Jesse's head-lights.

Realizing that she was still covered with Jesse's coat, Rennie's first instinct was to reach for the door handle and take it to him. If she was going to wait inside the car, the least she could do is let him wear it to keep dry while he conferred with the other driver.

She glanced in the back seat, hoping that Jesse kept an umbrella in the car like most Seattle drivers. No such luck. Rennie didn't relish the thought of getting out in the downpour to deliver the jacket, but she doubted Jesse would hear her if she tried to get his attention by rolling down her window and calling his name.

Judging by his lack of response to her question about his welfare, he seemed to have forgotten all about her. After all, a small voice in her mind whispered, he hadn't been worried about her well-being, either. Jesse had stormed into the rain out of fear for his beloved Beamer, not because he was concerned about either Rennie or the other driver.

Resolutely, she told the insistent voice to shut up. Jesse knew without looking that she was okay. The impact had been mild, more of a bump than anything. Before the little voice could come up with any other irritating remarks, she opened the door and stepped out into the chilling cold of the rain.

The shoulder of the road sloped steeply away from the edge of the pavement. Rennie had to hold on to the side of the car to keep from slipping down into the muddy stream of water that rushed along the road's edge. After a few perilous steps, she reached firmer ground between the two cars.

"Jesse," she called, "I've got your coat if you want it."

He was so intent on his conversation with the other driver that he didn't even glance in her direction. She called his name again, louder this time.

Still no response. As she stepped away from the BMW, she felt the first real stirrings of her temper. If he was at all concerned about her, she thought angrily, he'd have checked on her by now. As it was, she could have fallen in the ditch and drowned for all the attention he was paying to her.

Disgusted, she stalked over to where the two people were standing and thrust Jesse's jacket literally in his face.

"What the—" he stammered as he jerked around.

Rennie got her first clear view of Jesse's companion. The other person, looking miserable and dripping with rain, was an elderly lady.

"Excuse my rudeness, ma'am. I just thought he might like his coat since he obviously doesn't have the sense to get in out of the rain." Glaring at Jesse, she added, "Couldn't the two of you exchange information or whatever you're doing inside one of the cars with the engine running? At least that way you'd be warm."

"Sure, that'd be fine with me," the older woman spoke. "We can all fit in my car, if you'd like." She opened the passenger door of her car and got in, apparently assuming that Jesse and Rennie would follow.

Instead of joining Jesse and his companion, Rennie had chosen to go back to the BMW and wait. Perhaps another twenty minutes passed before Jesse opened the door and slid into his seat.

"You okay?" he asked as he turned the key in the ignition.

"Fine," came her terse response. The chilly tone of her voice gave lie to her answer.

Still suffering the aftereffects of the near brush with disaster, Jesse wasn't going to play guessing games about what was bothering Rennie. Without saying another word, he checked his mirrors for traffic. When Mrs. Swan, the owner of the other car, had successfully maneuvered back into traffic, Jesse watched for another break in the steady stream of cars and pulled out into the nearest lane.

They traveled in uneasy companionship for a couple of miles before the extended silence began to prey on Jesse's nerves.

"Is something wrong?" he finally asked with a quick glance at Rennie.

"Not so *you'd* notice," she unclenched her jaw long enough to answer.

The slight emphasis on the word *you* left Jesse puzzled.

"Look, are you upset about something? If so, tell me what it is. I'm not in the mood for twenty questions." This time, he didn't bother to check her reaction.

"Well, other than you never even bothered to ask me if I was hurt when that other car bumped into ours, I guess I'm just fine. Thank you for asking, even if it is a bit late to be worrying about it."

Instantly contrite, Jesse reached out and put his hand on her shoulder. "I'm sorry, Rennie. I just assumed you were okay or you'd have said something. Are you sore or anything? Should we stop at an emergency room?" His brown eyes, gentle with concern, quickly checked her from head to toe, looking for signs of injury or blood.

"No life-threatening injuries, if that's what you want to know. The impact was so slight, I almost thought I'd imagined it." She was staring out the passenger window with her arms folded across her chest.

Jesse's own temper started to fray around the edges. He took a deep breath and tried again.

"Then what are you mad about?"

"Nothing." She still wouldn't look at him.

"Nothing, my foot! It's so cold in here right now, I'd be warmer standing outside in the damn rain!" He stifled the urge to start yelling.

She slowly looked around to face him, sarcasm dripping from every word out of her mouth. "I'm surprised you're not still out in the rain, checking your precious Beamer for scratches or maybe even, horror of horrors, mud splashes." Her eyes had darkened to the same shade of gray as the rain-laden clouds hovering overhead.

"Just what are you insinuating, Rennie?" His barely contained fury was threatening to overwhelm him.

"I'm not insinuating anything, Jesse. I'm just pointing out the fact that this car of yours means more to you than I do. Or anybody else, for that matter."

"How so?"

"When normal people have an accident," she said haughtily, clearly indicating that he was not among that group in her opinion, "they check to see if everyone in the car is okay before worrying about a hunk of metal. They'd also think twice about leaving an elderly lady standing out in the rain, even if she did cause the accident."

"I already said I was sorry. Would it make you happy if I apologized again?"

"Don't bother. At this point, I wouldn't believe you anyway."

"Why not?" he demanded.

"Because Robin never meant it when he apologized, either. Not when he was late, not when he forgot our anniversary, not even when he missed seeing Becky born. You see, unfortunately she chose to come into this world while the stock market was still open." Rennie blinked her eyes rapidly, as if she were trying to prevent herself from crying.

"That's just what I'm talking about. You're punishing me for his mistakes." He was clutching the steering wheel so tightly, his hands ached.

"Yeah, well, when you act just like he did, it's hard not to," she retorted.

"Dammit, woman! When are you going to get it through your thick head that I'm not your husband?" He was yelling now.

"Thank goodness for that!" she snapped back. "Besides, I never said you were."

"Well, here's something else for you to be grateful for—I'm never going to be, either!" Then he added, "Or anyone else's, for that matter." With that enigmatic comment, he stopped talking and stared straight ahead at the road.

After struggling to regain control of his temper, Jesse decided that for the time being he'd better concentrate on his driving. They were getting into more populated areas and traffic was heavy. Shortly, he reached their exit off the highway and within minutes he was stopped in Rennie's driveway.

With a sigh, he turned off the ignition and leaned back against the headrest and closed his eyes. After a minute he looked at Rennie. She was studiously examining her hands which were folded in her lap.

"What now, Rennie?"

She glanced up, her eyes large and vulnerable. "I don't know. I guess I should just go in the house. You don't need to walk me to the door." She reached for the handle, then glanced back at him and added, "Bye, Jesse."

Her words had a finality to them that frightened him.

"Wait," he said. "Please."

She sat back in her seat again and waited for him to continue.

"Look, maybe we both overreacted today," he said.

She raised her eyebrows in response, a bare hint of a smile on her lips.

"All right, I definitely overreacted, but I think you did, too, even if it was mostly my fault." He frowned as he tried to sort out his feelings.

"I really enjoyed today, at least until the drive home. I'd hate to see us stop seeing each other over something stupid like this." He reached out and gently brushed his fingers along her face.

Her eyes reflected something he might think was regret. "I don't think it was stupid, Jesse. I think it was just a clear reminder of how different our values are."

"What values?"

"I value people more than things. I'm not sure you do." Her voice was sad.

Jesse's temper was back. "Rennie, I warned you once I wouldn't be judged by your husband's mistakes. If you can't look at me and know that family and friends are more important to me, then maybe it's better that we don't see each other." He couldn't resist adding, "If this is how you treated Robin all the time, I don't wonder he stayed away from home as much as he could."

Rennie gasped and rushed out of the car without another word. Wishing he could take back his hasty words, Jesse watched as she fumbled in her purse for her key. Then she was out of sight and out of his life.

Nine

Rennie washed the last of the dinner dishes and stacked them in the drainer to dry. This late in the spring in the Northwest, the sun set later and later. Even though it was time for Becky to be getting ready for bed, it was still light outside. Rennie stared out the kitchen window, lost in her thoughts.

"Mom, how come Mr. Daniels didn't come in tonight when he picked up Brittany from Trailblazers?" Becky asked, bringing Rennie back to her surroundings. "He just waited in the car until she noticed he was parked out front."

Hearing the concern in Becky's voice, Rennie turned from the window, forcing herself to smile. "Maybe he was tired, sweetie."

Becky thought about it, then said, "Brittany did say that he's had a headache since Sunday. Do you think he's sick or something?"

"Why are you so worried?" Rennie asked, afraid to hear the answer.

"Oh, no reason. Except it was sure fun having him around. You like him, too, don't you, Mom?" Becky's eyes were wide with innocent curiosity.

Rennie was no longer surprised at the stab of pain she felt every time Jesse crossed her thoughts. She tried to sound neutral when she answered. "Yes, honey, I like Mr. Daniels."

"Me, too. Maybe he'll come back when his head feels better." With that Becky finished her snack and headed upstairs to read a while before lights-out.

Rennie put the last of the leftovers in the refrigerator just as the phone rang. The noise startled her, causing Rennie to drop her favorite casserole dish on the floor. Gingerly she tiptoed around the shards of glass and spaghetti to reach for the phone.

"Hello," she said, and then cursed as she stepped on a fragment she'd missed seeing.

"Is that some new way to discourage telephone solicitors?" her mother-in-law asked. "I doubt it would work on most of them. Besides, you might just lose some friends that way."

Rennie laughed. "Guess I'll give it up then, because I've lost enough friends this week to last me a while." Realizing that she'd just revealed more than she'd meant to, she tried to change tactics. "What I meant was that I have few enough friends calling me this week as it is."

"Are we talking about any friend in particular?"

Hoping Madeline would be more easily distracted than normally, Rennie answered, "No, I'm just missing Vickie, I guess. Usually we talk several times during the week. It seems unnaturally quiet around here."

"What's the matter? I thought that nice-looking brother-in-law of hers was filling in rather nicely. Haven't you heard from him since Sunday?"

"Well, I did see him once." That wasn't exactly a lie, technically. She saw the back of his head earlier as he drove away from her house when he came for Brittany.

"So, are you going to see him again?" Madeline sounded determined to hear every last detail about Rennie's relationship with Jesse.

"No," Rennie sighed. She pulled a chair out and flopped down on it, giving in to the depression she'd been fighting since Sunday.

"Any particular reason?" Madeline asked, concern and curiosity equally mixed in her voice.

"None, except for the fact that we have differing values that made it impossible for us to have any kind of relationship." Rennie closed her eyes to suppress the sudden burning of tears in her eyes. She would not, absolutely would not, cry again.

"Rennie, dear, I know that it's really none of my business," Madeline started to say.

"That's never stopped you before," Rennie interrupted, humor easing the sting of the words.

"Yes, well, be that as it may, I'd like to ask you one thing: How could two intelligent people make a decision like that on the basis of one date?" Madeline sounded confused. "Did you find out something dreadful about him? Don't tell me he snores all night!"

"Madeline Sawyer! How could you ask me something like that? Besides, how would I know what he does all night?"

"Just wishful thinking, I guess. He seemed like such a nice sort that I guess I was hoping he'd be the one to break you out of your celibate lifestyle." Before Rennie could respond to that comment, Madeline continued. "Just what did break up the two of you?"

"It's like I said, just a case of differing values."

"Which values?"

"I care about people and he cares about his car."

Madeline responded with a pithy comment that Rennie had never heard her use before. "Let's just say that in my opinion, the way Jesse was looking at you Saturday wasn't exactly the same way he looked at his car."

"I'm sorry if you don't agree." Rennie responded. "I just think if two people are to have any chance at making a go of it these days, they'd better have more in common than raging hormones." She hoped that her words didn't sound as empty to her mother-in-law as they did to her.

"Even if what you say is true, what happened that made you come to this conclusion?"

"He didn't ask me if I was okay when we were involved in a minor accident on the way home Sunday."

"Were you okay?"

"Yes, but that's beside the point."

"No, I think it's exactly the point. You've been running away from men ever since Robin died because you're afraid you might end up with another husband who worships the almighty dollar more than he does you. You finally meet a man that most women would die for and you jump on the first excuse you could to head for the hills." Madeline had never before spoken in such harsh tones to Rennie.

"That isn't fair!"

"No, and neither is life, Rennie. Do you feel better now that you got rid of the man?"

"Whose side are you on? Mine or his?" Rennie demanded.

"I'm on whichever side will make you happier in the long run. If you're better off without Jesse, fine. If not, then maybe you need to do some serious thinking before writing him off so quickly."

* * *

Jesse stared at the telephone on the bedside table. Twice he had reached for it, and twice he had stopped before he picked up the receiver. Once he even dialed the number but disconnected the call before it could ring at the other end.

Damn, it just shouldn't be this hard! A man likes a woman; she seems to like him back. How could it get so complicated? He was even hiding from Brittany and Lexi up in his bedroom. Carrying his laptop computer up the stairs, he'd told them he was under the gun on a contract. They'd promised not to bother him unless a major crisis erupted.

He had no intention of even turning on the computer. If he worked up his courage to call Rennie, he just didn't want the girls listening in. Especially if he had to resort to begging the woman to go out with him. After all, a man had to maintain some semblance of dignity in front of his family.

He stared at the phone, wishing his normally decisive mind hadn't chosen this moment to turn into mush. The simple truth was that he missed Rennie so much it hurt. In just a few short days, the entire focus of his life had shifted, putting her right smack in the middle of all of his plans and dreams.

He sometimes had wondered if he was attracted only to women who were too busy or too shallow to want a long-term relationship. He'd even suspected that there was something lacking in his makeup that made him a poor choice for commitment. Always before, when a relationship had ended, it had been at most an inconvenience, leaving him without an escort to business functions.

This time, though, he wasn't going to give up without a fight. Rennie was too important to him. Just last night, he'd caught a quick glimpse of her when he'd picked up Brittany. It had taken all of his willpower to drive away.

He wanted her to let him try one more time. He needed her to let him back into her world. Glancing at the alarm clock on the dresser, he knew he couldn't stay locked in his room much longer. It was getting on toward dinnertime, and the girls would be getting hungry.

Resolutely he picked up the receiver again and punched in the numbers indelibly etched in his mind. One ring, two, then three. *Please, please answer,* he thought. *I may not be able to bring myself to try again. Please answer.*

On the fourth ring, Rennie answered. Her voice sounded slightly husky over the phone. His heart pounded so loudly, he was sure she could hear it over the line.

"Hello, yourself," Jesse stammered, hoping he sounded more confident than he felt.

"Jesse," she whispered.

For an eternity of seconds, neither of them spoke.

Finally, he tried again. "Are you speaking to me, or are you going to hang up right away?"

"No, Jesse, I won't hang up," she answered. "Is there something you wanted?"

"Mostly, I just wanted to talk to you."

"About what?"

"About us."

Her long sigh echoed in his ear and in his heart. "There is no us, Jesse. I thought we'd already decided that."

"Look, Rennie, I don't want to throw away all that we had on the basis of one car ride. And please, let's not make a decision like this over the phone."

He knew very well from his law practice that it was far harder for clients to turn down an offer when he was face-to-face with them. He hoped it would be more true for Rennie.

On impulse, he asked her, "Can we go somewhere to talk in private?"

"Jesse . . ." she pleaded.

She hadn't refused him outright. He pressed his advantage. "It can be anywhere that you want. Here at Vickie's, although we'd have the girls listening in. If we can get a baby-sitter, we could go to my place."

"No, not your place," she said firmly.

He had her on the run. "The beach?"

There was a brief silence. Finally, Rennie sighed. "Okay, but what are you going to do with the girls?"

"I didn't think that far ahead. Do you think the girls would be okay for a while on their own?"

"Why don't you bring them over here. My mother-in-law is due to come by in about an hour. I'm sure she'd stay with them for us."

"Great! We'll be there." He could hardly contain his excitement. "I'd better make them some dinner before we come, so I'll let you go for now." He gently set down the receiver and added to himself, "But not for long, Rennie Sawyer."

Jesse glanced at his image in the dresser mirror. He'd already lost that hangdog look he'd had when he'd first come upstairs. Did he have time for a quick shower? He'd make time.

Minutes later he was staring at his wardrobe, wishing he'd brought more of his clothes from home. Although it was spring, it got pretty chilly down by the water late in the evening. He finally settled on some black jeans and a sweater done in black, dark red, and white.

Vickie had told him that he looked drop-dead handsome in it when she had given him the sweater for his last birthday. He trusted her judgment in such matters. If he was a little overdressed for the beach, too bad. He wanted every advantage he could muster.

Now for dinner. He positively skipped down the steps, his excitement growing by the minute. He cheerfully broke the news to the girls that they were going to spend the evening at Becky's. They followed him into the kitchen to set the table while he grabbed a casserole out of the freezer and stuck it in the microwave.

He caught the girls giving him odd looks when he started singing a love ballad, but he didn't care. He quickly prepared a fresh green salad and sliced some French bread. Jesse had dinner on the table in record time. He had no idea how anything tasted. He just wanted to get the meal over with.

"Leave the dishes, girls. I'll do them later."

Shocked, Brittany stared at him in amazement. He had never let them slack off on chores before. Lexi didn't question her good luck since it was her week to wash. She just hurriedly carried her plate to the counter and beat a hasty retreat.

"Get your jackets and wait for me in the car."

Jesse checked the back door to make sure it was locked and was heading for the front when the phone rang. Fearing it might be Rennie changing her mind, he almost ignored it. After he answered it, he really wished he had.

"Mrs. Billings, what can I do for you?"

"I need more candy tonight, Mr. Daniels."

Jesse clenched his teeth, trying to keep his answer civil. "I'm sorry, but you caught me on the way out the door. It'll have to wait until tomorrow." His tone would have told anyone who knew him that he meant exactly what he said.

Mrs. Billings, however, didn't recognize determination when she heard it.

"But, Mr. Daniels—"

Jesse broke in. "I'm sorry, Mrs. Billings, but I'll talk to you about it in the morning." He hung up none too gently and made it out the front door just as the phone started ringing again.

Jesse forced himself to remember that he was driving through a residential area and controlled his urge to speed. After all, there were only a couple of blocks between him and Rennie. Even that was too far tonight.

She was at least willing to listen to him. That had to mean something.

Brittany was out of the car and at the front door before Jesse had even set the brake. He and Lexi followed at only a slightly more leisurely pace. Becky met them at the door.

She looked up at Jesse. "Hi! Mom's on the phone, so she told me to let you in." Turning to her friends, she exclaimed, "Hey, Brit, guess what? Grandma rented us the new Disney movie to watch! She ran to the store for popcorn and said we can even have root beer floats later!"

All three girls went off chattering toward Becky's bedroom. Jesse didn't feel abandoned. He was too intent on locating Rennie. He found her in the kitchen on the phone. Her next words told him who was on the other end of the line even though he could hear only half of the conversation.

"No, Mrs. Billings, I can't get any candy for you tonight . . . No, I don't know where he can be reached."

Jesse had to choke back a laugh at that. "Liar!" he mouthed to Rennie. She ignored him.

"Now, I'm sure he didn't mean to be rude. Mr. Daniels just isn't like that."

"Yes, I am," he whispered. Rennie elbowed him in the ribs.

"No, I am sorry, Mrs. Billings, but there's nothing I can do on such short notice. You should call ahead if you want more candy, because Mr. Daniels is a busy man. He can't stick around the house just in case we need him to hand out more chocolate."

Jesse slipped his arms around Rennie's waist and murmured in her ear, "I'd give you all the candy you want, little girl." He gave a lecherous chuckle and nuzzled her neck.

Rennie's voice cracked when she tried to talk to her caller again. "I'm, uh, sorry, Mrs. Billings, but someone's at the door. Have a nice evening." She hung up and whirled around to face her tormentor.

"Listen, buster, don't ever do that to me again!" She threatened him with her fist.

He backed off with his hands up in surrender. "You don't like me to hug you?"

"Don't be an idiot. Don't ever sic that woman on me again!"

Jesse had to laugh. "I'm sorry, I didn't know she'd call you this time. I made the mistake of answering the phone on my way out the door. If she weren't quite so pushy, I probably would have offered to leave some cases out on the porch for her. She just caught me when I had more important things on my mind."

The look in his brown eyes left little doubt what those things were.

"My mother-in-law should be back in just a minute. She ran to get some treats for the girls. Even though it's a school night, she figured a few extras wouldn't hurt them." Rennie moved away from Jesse. She busied herself with rinsing the last of the dinner dishes. "You know, she was pretty excited about your coming over."

"I'm glad that someone is on my side." Jesse resisted the urge to close the distance between them. If Rennie needed some space, he didn't want to push it.

"There's no sides to this," she chided. "We're just going for a walk on the beach."

Before he could respond, Madeline came through the front door. Jesse hurried to take the grocery sack she was carrying.

"Make note of that, Rennie. He's not only good-looking, but he has good manners, too."

"Madeline, quit pushing. The man has no problems with his ego as it is." Rennie gave both of her laughing guests a stern look. "You two behave while I go get my jacket and tell Becky good-bye." She walked away without a backward glance.

Madeline waited until she was down the hall before speaking to Jesse. "Mind your manners with her, young man. I don't know how you talked her into letting you see her again, but it wouldn't take much to scare her off."

"I know. I promise to take it easy. I just couldn't let things end the way they did."

Before he could say any more, Rennie was back. "It's a school night, so we won't be late, Madeline."

"Don't hurry on our account. The girls and I will be just fine."

Jesse led Rennie out to his car and opened the door for her. The drive to the beach took only about ten minutes. Soon they were strolling down the rocky beach, for the moment just enjoying the sights. The Sound was fairly smooth, and evening fishermen were out in their small boats. The commuter ferry was just docking at the nearby pier, bringing cars and passengers back to the mainland from Whidbey Island.

Suddenly, Jesse stopped, intently watching the water just off shore. "Look, there's a sea lion playing out there."

It took a second for Rennie to catch sight of the sleek animal frolicking in the chilly water.

"I've lived near the Sound my whole life, and I still never tire of watching for the seals," she told Jesse. "I've always meant to go on one of the whale-watching cruises when the orcas are around. Have you ever gone?"

"No, but I'd like to." Jesse knew Rennie felt more comfortable keeping the conversation on safe topics. For the moment, he let her.

Finally, when they'd reached a relatively unpopulated portion of the beach, he chose a driftwood log and sat down. Rennie joined him, careful to leave a small distance between them.

He stared out at the water for a while, tossing small stones into the incoming waves. Without glancing at her, he said, "Thanks for letting me come over tonight. I know it wasn't an easy choice for you."

"Well, after all the nagging my daughter and mother-in-law have been doing the last few days, I almost had to."

Jesse turned to look at her, his brown eyes hurt and a little tentative. "I'm sorry, Rennie, if you feel like you were forced to come."

"I said 'almost had to,' Jesse. If I hadn't wanted to come, I wouldn't be here. The truth is that I've missed you more than I would've thought possible."

A smile lit up his face. "I've never felt this way about anyone, Rennie." He held up his hand when she started to protest. "I know that it's hard to believe that in thirty-two years, I've never been in—"

At that point, she did interrupt. "No, don't say it, Jesse. It's too soon. Besides, I can't believe that you've never had a serious relationship before now."

"It's true. I've dated women, a couple for several months, but nothing ever came of it. Sometimes it was their choice, sometimes mine. I was too busy busting my britches working my way through college and then law school. Once I graduated, I had loans to pay off. There's just never been much time to concentrate on my personal life. Relationships need time and energy to work."

He laced his fingers through hers and held her hand trapped between both of his larger ones. "Until now, I've never met anyone I thought was worth the effort to try."

"What about Vanessa?" Rennie asked.

"Don't you mean Buffie?" Jesse teased. "Seriously, I already explained that we were convenient dates for each other. That's all."

Rennie sat quietly. "What now, Jesse? What do you want from me? I still think that we have too many differences to overcome."

"What differences? How can I deal with them when I'm not sure what they are."

"Our lifestyles for one thing. One great big thing. I've already been through one hellish marriage where a career was all that mattered." She stood and walked toward the water. She looked back at Jesse and spoke, "Our worlds are so far apart. I can't live in yours, and you'd never be happy in mine."

Jesse caught up with her and grabbed her arm, forcing her to face him. "Whoa, there. I've been living in your world for the last week. Now, while I'll admit that's not very long, I think I've done pretty well for a rank beginner. I also know how Mark and Vickie live. If that's what you're talking about, I'd give anything to have it that good."

Doubt was written all over her face. He continued, "I don't think your world, as you call it, is the real problem, is it? It's my world you're worried about. What do you want me to say, that I'll give up everything that I've worked for?" He was so frustrated that his words were taking on an angry edge. He had to stop before he blew what could be his last chance to get through to her.

They walked in silence for a few minutes. Jesse tried again. "I don't see why you think it has to be one way or the other. I can compromise and you could, too, if you're willing to try."

"I spent most of my marriage doing all the compromising," Rennie snapped. "I'm not going to do it again."

"Dammit, Rennie, I've told you before that I am not Robin. His mistakes are not my mistakes. He had it all and was stupid enough to throw it away. If I had what he had, I'd be holding on to it with all my strength." He was angry now and didn't care if Rennie knew it. "Quit convicting me of crimes I haven't committed."

Tears glistened in her eyes. "What do you want of me, Jesse?"

"I've tried your world and liked it. I want a chance to prove that my world isn't so bad. That's all I ask, Rennie. Give us a chance."

She walked away from him. After a few steps, she turned back. "Okay, one chance. Madeline says I'm not being fair to either of us if I refuse to see you again. The truth is that you scare me, Jesse. You could hurt me so very badly. After all I went through with Robin, I think I have a right to be cautious."

Jesse knew he'd better take what he could get. "We'll do this any way that you want. You set the rules and I'll live by them."

"I'll give you a chance to show me your world, Jesse. One chance."

Jesse whooped and grabbed Rennie around the waist, swinging her around. "Great! You won't regret this, honey. I promise." He set her back down and gave her a quick kiss. "Where do we go from here?"

"How about the lighthouse?" Rennie asked, pointing down the beach. "It's near where we parked and we should start heading back."

Together they walked toward the impeccably maintained lighthouse on the edge of the beach. Hand in hand, they strolled, content for the moment to enjoy each other's company. When they reached the end of the path, Jesse tugged Rennie toward him. She went willingly into his arms, not caring if the beach wasn't the most private of spots.

For a few seconds, he just held her close, her head snuggled against his chest. Her arms encircled his waist tightly. He hoped the warmth of his embrace would take away the chill of the evening air and the fears from her heart.

"Rennie," he whispered.

She looked up, her gray eyes stormy. Somehow, he had to remove the doubts he saw still lurking there. If his embrace wasn't enough, maybe his kiss would be.

He gave it his best shot.

"Quit fussing, Rennie! You look perfect and any more will just ruin it." Madeline grabbed Rennie's makeup bag from the counter and held it out of her reach.

"Don't you think I need just a touch more eye shadow?" Rennie asked, fully aware how nervous she sounded.

"No, enough is enough," Madeline admonished. "I've told you once and I'll tell you again: You look beautiful. Jesse would be the first to tell you that if you'd come out of the bathroom long enough for him to see you."

"He's here? Oh, gosh, am I late?" Rennie raced out of the bathroom and began frantically searching for her shoes. She started to get down on her hands and knees to check the back of the closet when Madeline stopped her.

"Honey, here they are. Remember—you put them on the dresser with your purse so you'd know where they were?" The older woman took Rennie by the arm and led her to the chair in the corner. "Sit. I'll get your shoes while you try to calm down. Its only a dinner party. It's not like you've never been to one before."

"But this one is so important, Maddy."

"Yes, well," Madeline said, shaking her head. "I've already told you what I think about that. How could you pin your future happiness on the outcome of one evening, Rennie Sawyer? Heaven forbid! What happens if the food isn't quite up to your standards? Or worse yet, someone has on the same dress that you're wearing? What then? Sorry, fella, it's all over?" She handed Rennie the shoes. "You're smarter than that. And if you aren't, that man, who's wearing a hole in your living room carpet right this minute, ought to be.

"Now come on out of here and get going. You relax and have a nice time. There's no one at that party who is better than you are." She tugged Rennie up out of the chair.

Rennie stopped long enough to give Madeline a quick kiss on the cheek. "Thanks for your vote of confidence. I'll need it if Vanessa is there."

"That woman must have ice in her veins if she let a man like

Jesse get away from her that easily. Keep in mind that he's with you because he wants to be."

Together they stepped out into the hallway. Madeline dropped back at the last minute to allow Jesse to have a clear view of Rennie. The look on his face made any verbal compliments redundant.

"Rennie," he said with hushed awe as he stared at her from across the room. Her hair was done up in an elegant chignon, emphasizing her graceful neck. Her dress, a floor-length black sheath, left one shoulder and arm bare. When she walked into the room, a slit on the side of the skirt gave him a tantalizing glimpse of her lovely long legs.

The nervous look in her eyes stirred him into action. He gave her a smile that was meant for her alone. He took her hands in his and gave her a gentle kiss. He was sorely tempted to deepen the embrace, but before anything else could happen, Madeline cleared her throat, reminding the two besotted adults that children were present.

"Girls, tell your mother and uncle good-night. If they have a lick of sense, they won't be home until long after you three are in bed asleep."

In short order, hugs and good-night kisses were distributed and Jesse was outside opening the car door for Rennie. Before she got in, he touched her face gently with the palm of his hand.

"Did I mention how very beautiful you are?"

Rennie shook her head.

"Never doubt it, my lady. If we were on our way to somewhere more private than my boss's house, I'd offer you some more convincing evidence. For now, this will have to do."

His kiss was still gentle, but its effect on both of them was electric. He teased the corners of her mouth with his tongue, asking for entry. She sighed, letting him lead the way.

He had to stop or die on the spot. He abruptly ended the kiss and, resting his forehead on hers, caressed her neck with a shaky hand. "Aw, honey, I wish we could just stay home tonight."

Rennie's answering chuckle was a little breathless. "If we're going to stay and watch Disney movies and eat popcorn with the girls, we're a bit overdressed, don't you think?"

"Tell me this," he said, as he helped her into the car. "How could seeing you overdressed make me think of nothing but seeing you undressed?"

Before Rennie could respond, he'd shut the door and was walking around to his side of the car.

"No, thanks, I'm fine," Rennie assured the white-jacketed waiter. She'd been nursing the same glass of champagne for an hour. About the same amount of time since she'd last seen Jesse.

Taking a deep breath, she forced herself to move out of the corner where she'd been more or less hiding for the past fifteen minutes. For a while she'd tried making polite conversation with various people. Unfortunately, she was one of the few at the party who didn't know everybody else. There were only so many things she could think of to say to people she didn't know.

She'd just overheard the hostess say dinner was imminent. Rennie decided to find Jesse to remind him that he had a dinner date before everyone made the official exodus into the dining room. The crowning glory of an already miserable evening would be having to eat alone at a table full of strangers.

She finally caught sight of him standing with a group of people in the far corner near the fireplace. It took some doing to maneuver carefully between the clusters of guests scattered across the enormous room.

She tried not to be angry with Jesse for leaving her alone, but she didn't succeed. Coming to the party had been hard enough for her without having to be on her own for so long. They'd been standing with a large group of people when his boss had found them. He had explained that he needed to borrow Jesse for a few minutes because a major new client for the law firm was asking to meet him. It wasn't Jesse's fault that without him Rennie felt adrift in the room.

Just as she reached the other side of the room, Jesse caught her eye and smiled. He was talking to an older couple and Fred Pace, who was his boss and their host, and Vanessa. Jesse made room for her next to him without missing a word of the conversation. The only clue she had that he was really aware of her presence was when he casually put his hand around her waist. During a brief lull, he quickly made introductions.

"Everyone, I'd like to present Rennie Sawyer." Turning to face her, he continued, "Rennie, this is Mr. and Mrs. Tennyson. You've already met Fred, and I'm sure you remember Vanessa."

Obviously, the other woman hadn't immediately recognized Rennie. Now that she did, she wasn't happy at all to see Rennie by Jesse's side.

"Oh, yes. We met the other night outside the mall. Tell me, Ms. Sawyer, how is your little candy sale going?" Without giving Rennie a chance to answer, the elegant blonde turned to the Tennysons, effectively excluding Rennie from the conversation. "You should've seen it. Jesse was being such a good sport helping his nieces sell Trailblazer candy because Ms. Sawyer couldn't handle it alone."

Rennie gritted her teeth to keep from screaming. The gentle pressure of Jesse's hand on her arm told her that he was fully aware of her anger.

"I explained to you then, Vanessa, that Rennie was being kind in sharing her allotted time at the mall with my nieces." For the sake of the Tennysons, he added by way of explanation, "I'm staying with the girls for two weeks while my brother and his wife take a long-deserved vacation. I'm not sure I'd have survived it without Rennie's help." The warmth in his eyes made his smile seem like it was for Rennie alone.

Her blue eyes twinkling, Mrs. Tennyson spoke up. "When our girls were small, I headed up the candy sale for their clubs twice, and I've never worked so hard. I learned from the experience, though. Since then, the banquets and auctions I've had to organize have seemed like a picnic."

Then, bless her heart, she met Vanessa's startled gaze with a slight frown. "Never underestimate the amount of energy and dedication it takes to be a good parent, young lady. A job is all well and good, but a successful career is pretty cold comfort when you get to be my age."

There was nothing Vanessa could say to that. She obviously couldn't risk offending the Tennysons. The situation could have become awkward, but just then Mrs. Pace joined them.

"Excuse me for interrupting, but dinner is ready to be served. Fred and I had better lead the way before it gets cold."

The Tennysons followed their hosts out of the living room. Jesse and Rennie hung back briefly, waiting for the crush of guests to be seated. Finally, Jesse and Rennie chose seats at one of the smaller tables.

The conversation flowed around them. Rennie wondered if her

stomach would relax enough to let her enjoy the meal. It was doubt-ful.

Jesse leaned close and whispered, "See, honey, this isn't as bad as you thought it would be."

No, it's worse, she thought to herself. To Jesse, she just smiled. One of the other attorneys from his firm joined their table with his wife, a CPA for the same company. Rennie let Jesse do most of the talking, making a comment only when absolutely necessary. She felt so out of her element, it hurt.

She tried telling herself that she was being silly, that all her doubts and misgivings were left over from her marriage. Robin would never have defended her the way that Jesse had. That had to count for something, but that didn't change the fact that she felt out of place.

Her biggest regret of the evening was that her last time with Jesse had to be such a public forum. Maybe it was best, though, because when they were alone, it was too easy to forget that this was his true environment. All it took to know that was one glance at Jesse's ani-mated face as he good-naturedly argued with his co-workers about the best way to word a new contract under the most recent tax laws.

Course by course, the dinner passed. Finally, in a flurry of activity, the waiters served peach flambé, an elegant ending to the evening.

Rennie's heart ached as she watched the fine brandy burn, certain that her relationship with Jesse was going up in flames as well.

Ten

Jesse knew something was dreadfully wrong even before they left the party. After dinner, Rennie had discussed at length the current hot issues regarding public education with a woman from his office. On the way out, she'd made all the proper noises to their hosts about the lovely time she'd had. For all appearances, she had enjoyed herself.

But Jesse, who knew her better than she thought, hadn't been fooled. She was so tense he was afraid she would shatter.

Rennie was upset and that didn't bode well for the outcome of their experiment. She'd given him only one chance and he'd evidently blown it.

Looking back over the evening, he knew that he had left her alone for much too long. He doubted very much that she'd appreciate his explanation that he was used to being with Vanessa. Just as often, she was the one who went off by herself at one of these affairs.

Damn, what an idiot he'd been!

He'd tried so hard to convince her that he wasn't just like Robin, then proceeded to make himself out a liar the first chance he got. Instead of driving to her house, he pulled into the driveway at Vickie's. At the very least, he needed a few private minutes with her. He got out of the car to open her door for her. Without a word, she let him lead her into the house.

"I'll make some coffee." He quickly left the room. In just a short time, he was back. She was still standing where he'd left her.

She was staring out into the night, the set of her shoulders drooping and weary. So different from the beautiful, energetic woman she'd been just hours ago.

"I'm sorry, you know," he said softly as he walked up behind her.

She jumped as if he startled her out of a deep reverie.

"I'm sorry, did you say something?"

Sighing, Jesse tried again. "I said I was sorry, Rennie."

She wasn't going to give him an inch more than she had to. "For what?" she asked without looking at him.

"For everything. For nothing." Frustrated, he shoved his hands into his pockets. "Talk to me, Rennie. Look at me. Please give me at least that much."

Slowly, she did as he asked. Immediately, he wished she hadn't. Her eyes shimmered with tears yet unshed. There was such sorrow in them that he feared his heart would break with the pain of it all.

"You're not going to give me another chance, are you, Rennie?"

Her only answer was a lone tear coursing down her cheek. She started to turn back to the window. His hand shot out almost of its own accord and yanked her around.

"Quit avoiding me, Rennie. We have to talk this out, or we'll never get anywhere in this relationship." His temper, sparked by both guilt and frustration, was not far from exploding.

"What is there to say, Jesse? I was right and you were wrong. I can't fit into your world." Angrily, she wiped the tears from her face. "What I can't figure out is why I let myself get talked into even trying life in the fast lane again."

That was all it took. Jesse gave vent to his frustration. "What try, Rennie? You went into this evening prepared to be miserable."

"I did not!" she cried. "I gave it my best shot."

"So tell me, how much of the evening was so horrible? When did you start having a bad time? When I picked you up? When we reached the party? When I screwed up and left you alone too long?"

"Stop it, Jesse!"

"How about admitting that you actually liked several of the people you met? That maybe next time, if there is a next time, it would be easier for you to relax because you'd already know some of my friends. But, no, you couldn't possibly do that." He ran his fingers through his hair, wishing he knew how to salvage the evening.

"It wasn't like that," Rennie pleaded. "It wasn't." Her voice ended on a sob. "Take me home."

"No. If this evening is costing me my last chance to make a go of it with you, I want to know where I went wrong. Is it because of Vanessa? Was her being there enough to ruin the whole evening? I guess that nice Mrs. Tennyson didn't count for anything? Did it ruin your evening to find out that there was another woman in the room who understood the complexities of motherhood? After dinner, you and Margaret Jenkins looked awfully cozy talking about the school situation. Was that all a part of the miserable time you had?"

"Jesse!" she cried, shocked at his vehemence.

He stopped his tirade long enough to draw a ragged breath. "You know what I think. Just like I said, you went prepared to have a lousy time and you had one. Now you can retreat back into your safe little world telling yourself that you tried."

"That's just not true! That's not what happened!"

"Then tell me what went wrong."

Instead, Rennie jerked her arm free from his grasp. "I think you'd better take me home."

Mutely, he did as she asked.

Jesse stood at the window, studying the slow movement of clouds across the late-evening sky. The girls were firmly ensconced in front of the television in the family room watching one of their favorite movies. Their parents were due home in just over an hour, and Jesse had promised to let the girls stay up until Mark and Vickie got home.

He was too restless to enjoy the antics of two teenage boys on an escapade through time. Even the girls' giggling was grating on his nerves. Rather than take his bad mood out on them, he'd opted for the living room and his computer.

When even that couldn't occupy his mind, Jesse gave up and tried to soothe his nerves by enjoying the sunset. It had been almost a week since he'd done more than get a brief glimpse of Rennie, and he was missing her more than ever. At least early in the week, he'd had some leftover anger to sustain him. Now all he had left was an empty feeling—that and a headache.

He sat back down in front of his computer and forced his weary mind to absorb the information displayed there. Gradually, his awareness of his surroundings dimmed and he lost himself in the familiar territory of contract jargon.

"Well, isn't that just typical!"

The laughing voice of his brother jarred Jesse out of his computer trance. Somewhat guiltily, he looked around to find Vickie and Mark hugging their daughters and laughing at Jesse.

"Not all of us can afford two-week vacations in Hawaii, big brother," Jesse retorted. "I have to work for a living, you know." He joined the others and did his share of hugging.

"Well, do you like my tan?" Vickie asked as she pirouetted in front of Jesse, her blue eyes sparkling.

"You look rested and happy, Vic." Turning to his brother, he added, "The trip must have been good for you, too, because I do believe you have fewer gray hairs than you did before you left."

Mark punched him on the arm in response. "Tell us, did you survive two weeks of the kind of peace and quiet we have around here?"

Jesse rolled his eyes and shrugged. "Piece of cake. Takes more than being a Candy Dad to throw this attorney."

Gradually, they all moved into the kitchen and sat around the table. Mark handed out the souvenirs they'd brought back for Lexi, Brittany, and Jesse. While the girls oohed and aahed over their Hawaiian-style dresses, Jesse could only laugh at the loud floral shirt that Vickie had picked out especially for him.

"Gee, do you think hot pink and bright purple flowers are really me?" he asked, holding the shirt up in front of him. The answering laughs gave him his answer.

Shortly, with no little reluctance, Brittany and Lexi gathered up their treasures, preparing to head upstairs and their beds.

"Come give me a hug good-bye," Jesse said before they left the room.

"You going home this late?" Vickie asked as she poured him a cup of coffee. She sounded surprised. "Why not stay over and drive home in the morning?"

"Guess I'm just homesick," Jesse answered, hoping she'd accept his explanation. Seeing the doubt in her eyes, he added, "I also want to go into the office in the morning and catch up on some of my mail."

"On Sunday?" It was Mark questioning Jesse's motivation this time.

Vickie must have read the unhappiness in Jesse's face because she signaled Mark to let it pass. He left the room to check on the girls, leaving Vickie behind with his brother.

"Did something happen while we were gone?" she asked.

"You mean besides being attacked by Mrs. Billings and getting permanent hearing damage from listening to out-of-tune musical instruments?"

"Yes, besides those." She hesitated and then asked, "Was the candy a nightmare?"

"No, Rennie Sawyer helped me get it all under control. I'll be back next Friday to help you deal with all the final returns on candy and to count all the money. I've made sure that everything so far matches to the penny."

Despite his efforts to keep his voice neutral, Vickie must have picked up on something, because she pounced on his casual mention of Rennie's name.

"Tell me, what did you think of her?"

"Mrs. Billings is one pushy woman," he answered dryly.

"Not her, idiot. I meant Rennie," Vickie persisted.

Jesse's voice softened. "I liked her."

"Just liked her, or did you *really* like her?"

"Does it matter?"

"You tell me," Vickie answered, her eyes soft with growing concern.

Jesse stared into his coffee cup and gathered his thoughts. Vickie was the one person in the world he'd never been able to fool. He chose his words carefully.

"I think she's pretty special."

"Want to talk about it?"

"No, but you'll pry it out of me eventually, so I might as well." He crossed the kitchen and refilled his cup. "You sure you want to hear this after your long flight?"

"I'm all ears," came her reply.

"Besides meeting her the first night I was here, she helped me with the candy. We attended the band concert together and took the girls out for ice cream afterward. Next Rennie shared her time slot at the mall to sell candy with us, where we ran into Vanessa, who, by the way, is no longer speaking to me."

Vickie shrugged. "No great loss, if you ask me."

"I didn't," he said firmly. "The girls spent last Saturday night with your mom, so I helped Rennie spread bark in her yard. We went out for pizza afterward." He sat back down at the table and added milk and sugar to his cup before he continued. "We were both on our own Sunday, so we went up to Friday Harbor for the day. I took her to a dinner party at my boss's house Thursday night." His eyes bleak, he concluded, "That's about it."

With a worried frown, Vickie asked, "Any future plans?"

"She, I mean we, decided that our values are too different to make a relationship work."

His careful monotone didn't fool his perceptive sister-in-law. "And do you really believe that?"

Jesse sighed and looked up to meet Vickie's troubled gaze. "I believe Rennie Sawyer is every bit as special as you are. She'll make some lucky man a terrific wife."

"Any reason that man can't be you?"

Jesse couldn't bring himself to respond. Despite the short time he'd known Rennie, the pain of losing her was still acute. He stood to leave.

"Well, I'll be heading out now. Tell the girls bye for me." He planted a quick kiss on Vickie's cheek and headed for the front door, where his suitcase waited.

Before he even reached the hall, Vickie's angry voice stopped him cold.

"Damn you, Jesse Daniels!"

He turned back to face her, stunned not only by her tone, but by her language. She was practically vibrating she was so mad. She was standing with her hands on her hips, ready to take on the world if necessary to protect someone she cared about.

"What?"

"I'll bet you let her walk away just because you still have it in that thick skull of yours that you're not worthy of someone like Rennie. I realize that poor excuse of a mother you had managed to foist all of her own feelings of inadequacy off on you. However that is no reason to let her ruin your adult life like she did your child-hood!"

She took a breath and then started in again. For emphasis she'd stomped over to where Jesse stood with his mouth hanging open and began punctuating each word by poking him in the chest with her finger. "Let me tell you, buster, that you have more to offer than most women would know how to use!"

Jesse had to laugh at that. "Why, thank you, Vic, but how would you know that?"

"What? Oh, you!" She glared at his impudence and then gave in and smiled back. "You know what I meant and it wasn't that. You're well-educated, gentle, and loving. I'd tell you just how handsome you really are if it wouldn't go right to your head."

"Aw, geez, ma'am." Jesse did an imitation of a gawky boy, hanging his head and staring at his feet.

"Yes, well," Vickie continued, "I'm just tired of you selling yourself short. If you think Rennie's the woman for you, then you're going to have to go after her. She has a thing about three-piece suits, but you can get around that if you keep trying."

Jesse pulled Vickie close for a brotherly hug. "Thanks. Sometimes I forget to tell you how really wonderful you are for my poor battered ego."

"What are you going to do?"

"Well, right now I'm going home to get a good night's sleep. Then I'll start working on the problem. Maybe if I let her stew for another week or so, she'll realize how miserable she is without me."

Vickie walked him as far as the door. "Just as long as you don't give up without trying. I'll let you know when to come back to finish up the candy stuff. Maybe I can accidentally tell Rennie to bring her stuff when you're here." She gave him a conspiratorial wink.

"Glad you're on my side instead of hers," Jesse said as he headed out the door. "Let me know if you come up with any more strategies that'll help me lay siege to Rennie's defenses."

After he got into the car, he rolled down his window and called to Vickie as she watched from the porch, "I wouldn't even mind fighting dirty if it comes to that. I might even enjoy it."

He could hear Vickie laughing as he drove off into the night.

"And I thought I was a compulsive record keeper!" Jesse complained as he filled out yet another candy form.

"Quit complaining. At least we're on the home stretch on this stuff." Vickie was running a total on a column of numbers for the fourth time. "Do you think the Trailblazer office would notice if I just averaged the four answers I've gotten so far?"

Jesse gave that question all the consideration it was due—none.

He methodically double-checked all of his own answers and then set his stack of papers aside.

He tried to sound casual as he asked, "Are you sure Rennie is coming by tonight?"

"Yes, now don't interrupt me again." Vickie entered the last number, closed her eyes and hit the total button. Cautiously, she opened one eye and looked at the number illuminated on the calculator.

"I did it! I got the same number twice. I'm not going to press my luck by checking it again." She filled out the bottom of the form and tossed it on the stack by Jesse.

After glancing at her watch, she looked up at Jesse with a wide-eyed innocent expression on her face. "Gee, Jess. Rennie's due here in ten minutes and I just remembered that I've got to run to the store for something."

"What?"

"How should I know? I'll find out when I get there." She reached for her purse and dug out her keys. She looked at them thoughtfully and then dropped them back in. "Let me have the keys to the BMW," she demanded, holding out her hand to Jesse.

As he tossed them to her, he asked, "May I ask why, or is that too much to expect?"

Vickie rolled her eyes and spoke with exaggerated patience. "I worked hard to get Mark and the girls out of the house tonight. Now I'm going to make myself scarce. If Rennie sees your car, she might drive off without stopping. I'm just eliminating that possibility. It's up to you to make the most of this golden opportunity to worm your way back into her life."

Jesse laughed and went back to his paperwork. If his stomach was feeling the effects of his growing nervousness, he tried to ignore it. Still, he listened carefully for the sound of a car pulling into the driveway or a knock at the door.

About five minutes later, the doorbell rang. Jesse pushed away from the table and started toward the front door. He paused long enough only to check his appearance in the shiny chrome toaster sitting nearby on the kitchen counter and to wipe his hands on the dish towel in case his palms were sweaty.

He deliberately stood on the far side of the door when he opened it so that Rennie couldn't immediately see him. He figured if she had to step through the door she'd be unlikely to just hand him her club's candy money without staying. Jesse took a deep breath, pulled the door open, and waited for Rennie to walk back into his life.

Standing in the glare of the porch light, Rennie had trouble seeing clearly into the dark entryway of Vickie's house. At first she didn't see anyone, but then she caught the dark shape of a man standing just beyond the door.

"Mr. Daniels?" she asked.

"Don't you think it's a bit late for such formality between us, Rennie?"

"Jess? What are you doing here?" She hoped her voice didn't betray her shock. Or the sudden surge of happiness her traitorous heart felt.

Jesse opened the door wider and motioned her to come in.

"I'm the Candy Dad, remember?" His voice was friendly, his tone matter-of-fact.

Suddenly suspicious, Rennie asked, "I thought you were just filling in till Vickie got back to bail you out?"

As he led the way to the kitchen, Jesse spoke over his shoulder. "No. I started it and I'll finish it. Amazing, though, how much easier those forms get when someone who's done it all before is around to answer questions."

Rennie suddenly realized that she'd offered her help but hadn't even called to see if he was having problems. Though she'd made the deliberate, if painful, decision to avoid further involvement with the man, that was no excuse for deserting him mid-project.

"I'm sorry. I should have been here to help you before now."

"No problem," Jesse answered, smiling reassuringly. "I managed to get through Mrs. Billings's repeated trips for candy with only a minimum of wear and tear on my central nervous system. After her, all the other stuff's been a breeze."

He pulled a chair out for Rennie at the table and sat down across from her.

"Well, I'm sure you'd like to be done and rid of this mess. Here's my money and reports," she said, as she pushed a large envelope toward him. "The unsold candy is out in the van. I'm proud to say that the club sold all but twelve packages."

"What?" Jesse exclaimed in mock honor. "Mrs. Billings's club didn't return any. What's the matter with your bunch?"

Chuckling, Rennie retorted, "Mrs. Billings is a fanatic. Besides, if a certain uncle would like to spring for the last few, we could have a perfect record, too."

"Although trying to appeal to my family loyalty would work in most cases, it won't this time," Jesse said, shaking his head. "To tell you the truth, if I don't see another chocolate bar again until next year, that's just fine with me."

As he bent over the summary sheet and stack of bills and checks she'd given him, Rennie took the opportunity to study him. The light over the table brought out all the red highlights in his hair. She tried to concentrate on the candy sale but found herself wanting to reach out and brush back an errant lock of hair from his forehead. Or, better yet, to stand behind him and massage his broad shoulders to ease any stiffness he might be feeling from all the paperwork he'd been doing.

Anything to again touch Jesse's warmth and strength.

He must have felt her gaze, because he looked up for a second and smiled. She couldn't think of a thing to say, so she pretended an interest she certainly didn't feel in the candy brochure lying on the table. She'd been handing out the things for the last three weeks and knew the information it contained backward and forward.

She wondered if Jesse was feeling the same awkwardness she was. Probably not. Besides, that witch Vanessa might have wormed her way back into his life in the last week and been filling his time.

"How's Vanessa?" she blurted out, and felt a blush creep up her face.

"I wouldn't know," Jesse answered without looking up. There was nothing in his voice to indicate that he was upset by the fact or that he was surprised by the question.

Rennie, on the other hand, felt like grinning or maybe dancing around the room. Strange behavior for a woman who'd so sincerely resolved just a few days ago that Jesse Daniels had no place in her life.

In short order, he finished his report and handed the papers over for Rennie's signature. Once that was done, she had no reason to linger anymore. Especially since Jesse, although he was friendly and acted glad to see her, didn't seem particularly anxious to stop and chat with her once the work was finished.

She stood to take her leave.

"Thanks for all your work on this sale, Jesse. Even if we don't always remember to thank parents and their substitutes, we'd never be able to make Trailblazer work without their support."

"Oh, that's all right. I actually enjoyed it, but don't tell Mrs. Billings I said that," he added. "I'll follow you out to the van and carry in the candy for you."

"Glad you reminded me. I'd forgotten it was out there and I probably would've gone all the way home before I thought of it."

Together, they walked out to the driveway. She led the way to the back of the van and opened the door. She was aware of every breath Jesse took when he leaned in next to her to lift out the case of chocolate bars. Rennie stepped back out of his way, hoping he didn't notice how nervous she was.

When she ducked around the side of the van, Jesse allowed himself a devilish grin. The attorneys he faced in court would have recognized the smile—it was the one he gave them when he found his opponent's weakness and was about to move in for the kill.

Rennie was waiting by the driver's door. Jesse set the candy down and stepped closer to her. She must have read something in his body language because she tried to back away from him, only to find herself against the side of the van with no room to maneuver.

Without a word, Jesse closed the distance between them. His hands took control of her face, positioning it for the kiss he had every intention of giving her. She might not want him, might not trust him, but she was going to know him, in the most elemental way.

His lips touched hers, gently at first, giving her a last chance to protest, to escape. The only sound she made was one of surrender as her arms found their way around his waist.

He kissed her eyes, her neck, touched her throat with his tongue. And then he returned to her mouth, taking her lips and finding his way inside them. He pressed her against the van and rocked against her gently, letting Rennie taste the heat of his kiss and feel the strength of his passion.

Then, before she had a chance to protest, he ended the kiss. He opened the driver's door and helped a stunned Rennie into her seat. He gave her another gentle kiss on her cheek and caressed the dark silk of her hair.

"That's how I wish last Friday night had ended for us, Rennie."

As he shut her door, he paused before asking, "Still think we're wrong for each other?"

Then he calmly picked up the candy and walked away from her without looking back or waiting for her answer.

The second stage of Jesse's campaign to insinuate his way back into Rennie's life was about to be launched. This time, his plan of action was less direct because his target was Rennie's daughter and his unwitting accomplices were Brittany and Lexi.

It was Vickie, his co-conspirator, who had set the plan in action, extending a seemingly innocent invitation to Becky to accompany her two girls on an outing to the zoo. She waited until after Rennie had already agreed and told Becky before casually mentioning that it was Jesse who was taking the girls.

After a brief stop at Vickie's, he was on his way to Rennie's house to pick up Becky. He refused to feel guilty, although he supposed he should. If he and Rennie were ever going to have a chance at happiness together, he had to pursue her through whatever means were at his disposal.

He tried to act casual as he rang Rennie's doorbell. Becky immediately answered the door.

"Hi, Mr. Daniels. I'm all ready." She passed him at a run to join Brittany in the car. "Mom will be out in a minute."

He patiently waited until Rennie appeared. By the time she did, his hands were shaking. He quickly put them in his pockets to hide the telltale sign.

"Jesse."

"Hi, Rennie. Thanks for letting Becky go with us." He stood there awkwardly, unsure what to say next. "Well, I guess we'd better be going." He turned away, cursing himself for not being more smooth talking.

"What time do you think you'll bring her home?" Rennie called after him.

"After dinner sometime. The girls made me promise to hit the pizza place on the way back." Memories of the laughter Rennie and Jesse had shared at the same restaurant flashed through his mind.

The look on Rennie's face told him that she, too, was remembering. She flushed and ducked her eyes, avoiding his gaze.

"Uh, well, that'll be fine. It'll give me a chance to get caught up on some work." She stepped inside and softly shut the door.

Jesse was humming when he got into the car. The divine Ms. Sawyer wasn't immune to his presence. Score another point for his side.

Rennie tore the last report off of her printer and glanced at the clock. She still had at least an hour before Becky would be back from her outing with the Daniels girls. And with Jesse.

Not for the first time since they'd left, a surge of envy tore through her. How could a mature, level-headed woman possibly be jealous of her own eight-year-old daughter?

For Pete's sake, Rennie didn't even like the zoo all that much. Yet all afternoon, between medical reports and business letters, she'd pause, wondering where they were. Was Jesse charming the girls, teasing them into fits of giggles?

The scoundrel, he was probably spoiling them rotten with cotton candy and soda pop. At this very minute, the managers of the zoo stores were probably rubbing their hands with glee, watching the handsome man with the three darling girls buying out the place.

Shaking her head, she turned off the computer and put away the remnants of the afternoon's work. It was a sorry day when the worst thing she could think of about the man was that he was a nice guy, guilty only of being a pushover when it came to those he cared for.

If she thought too much about Jesse, the pain that haunted her since their breakup would come rushing back, strong as ever. Rennie looked around the kitchen, searching for something to occupy her mind. No luck.

She sat down in her favorite chair and tried to concentrate on the latest best-selling novel. She gave it up when the description of the hero sounded all too much like Jesse.

Why did the man have to be a part of the world that had caused her so much pain in the past? Why couldn't he be a plumber or an electrician or any other job that didn't move in the high-powered corporate world?

Because that wasn't who Jesse was, that's why, she admitted to herself. She had no right to want to change him, especially when he'd worked so hard to get where he was. In moments of brutal honesty, she could even admit that the problem wasn't with Jesse. She was the one with the problems, the insecurities, the paralyzing fears.

She tossed the book aside. Maybe a shower would help. Better yet, a hot bath with her favorite scented crystals. Resolutely, she marched back to her bathroom and turned the water on full blast.

She tied her hair up on top of her head and stepped into the soothing water, immersing herself up to her chin. She closed her eyes and felt the tension gradually leaving her. In the half-world between sleep and wakefulness, her mind wandered, allowing in the dreams that she had previously tried to deny herself.

In her mind's eye, the fateful dinner party took on a whole new look. Instead of the room being crowded with movers and shakers, couples whirled and danced to the strains of music from an age gone by. Jesse crossed the room to where she stood waiting and simply held out his hand.

Without hesitation, she put her hand in his, entrusted her heart to his keeping. Together they headed for the dance floor and moved as one to the intoxicating beat. Waltzes were written for lovers, and this dance was theirs.

Gradually, they separated from the others sharing the dance and stepped outside through double doors into a garden. For a while, they continued to dance, slowing gradually, finally ending the dance in a close embrace. In the moonlight, Jesse's kiss was intoxicating, sending chills up and down Rennie's spine. She could hear bells.

Bells! Rennie jumped up and grabbed a towel. The bell she was hearing was all too real. Someone was at the front door. With her luck, it was Becky trying to get in.

Rennie practically ran down the hall, tying her robe's belt snugly, all the while berating herself. How could she have lost track of time like that? If her suspicions were right, she was going to have to face Jesse in nothing more than her everyday robe.

Sure enough, she could see Becky peering in through the small window next to the door. Rennie turned the lock and let her daughter in. She looked out the window for Jesse. He was already pulling out of the driveway, waving as he drove off. Telling herself it was better that way, she turned her attention to Becky.

"Sorry, Becky, I lost track of time. I didn't mean to lock you out."

Becky, always willing to forgive and forget, hugged her mom and handed her a foil-covered plate.

"Mr. Daniels said to give you this. It's the leftover pizza. He thought you might not want to cook dinner just for yourself." Without pausing for breath, Becky chattered on. "Wanna see what all I brought home from the zoo?"

"Sure, honey, that would be great." The plate of pizza felt heavy in her hand, or maybe it was her heart that was feeling the weight. Her dream had left her unsettled; Jesse's abrupt departure even more so.

Becky sat down at the kitchen table and began to spread out all of her loot for her mother's inspection. While she arranged it all to her satisfaction, Rennie decided to heat the pizza. No use in letting good food go to waste.

She punched the buttons on the microwave and uncovered the plate. One look at the pizza and her heart skipped a beat, her hands shook. Jesse had sent her the pizza all right. He'd also sent her a reminder of the night they'd laughed over mushrooms and cheese: He'd neatly cut off the point of each piece on the plate, claiming his part of her meal. And maybe her heart.

Eleven

"Come on, Mom. Let's go!" Becky called, anxious to be off.

"I'm almost ready," Rennie assured her. "Why don't you go on ahead. I'll catch up in just a minute."

The sound of the door slamming made Rennie smile. Becky had been counting the hours until it was time for the neighborhood block party to begin. Rennie finished covering the bowl of potato salad she'd made for the occasion. She carefully arranged the cooler so that the salad wouldn't spill in transit. Next she added the sliced vegetables and dip.

She looked around the kitchen to see if she'd missed anything. No, she had the basket with their utensils, and the cooler was ready. That should do it.

She stopped in the bathroom to make a last-minute check on her appearance. Staring back at her from the mirror was the face of a woman in her early thirties looking less than delighted about having to go out for the afternoon. At least superficially, she looked good.

She'd pulled her dark hair back with clips, letting it fall down to her shoulders in a casual style. And even she had to admit that her peach-colored jacket and matching pants were perfect for her coloring. Another touch of lipstick and she was at last ready to join in the festivities. At least, that's what she kept telling herself.

In truth, she'd been in no mood for the company of others and hadn't been since last weekend when Jesse had again intruded into her life. Only at Becky's insistence had she agreed to attend the annual event.

She put her keys in her pocket to avoid carrying a purse. She picked up the basket and cooler and walked out the front door. After pulling the door closed behind her, she headed out toward Vickie's house, where the barbecue was being held this year.

The year before was the first block party she'd attended. Always before that, Robin had had more important things to do than associate with the neighbors. Vickie had been there alone, too, because Mark had been out of town. The two women had spent the afternoon talking while keeping a watchful eye on their children.

This year, Rennie had some serious misgivings about going. She wasn't sure how Vickie felt about Rennie and Jesse's situation. It was all Rennie could do not to call her friend and pour out all of her problems, but she didn't want to put Vickie in such an awkward position.

She also wasn't sure whose side Vickie would be on if push came to shove. Probably Jesse's, since he was family, after all. Looking back, Rennie had to admit that it had been more than a little suspicious that Vickie had invited Becky to the zoo without first mentioning that it was Jesse who would be driving.

When Rennie turned down Vickie's street, she immediately scanned the parked cars for one belonging to a certain attorney. She gave a mental sigh of relief when she didn't see the familiar vehicle anywhere. It had crossed her mind that he might be at the party since the get-together was being held at his brother's home.

She walked around the side of the house. Already the kids and some of the adults were playing a hot game of volleyball. She scooted past the net, heading toward the back. Smoke from the barbecue hung in the air, making her mouth water.

"Want help with those?"

Rennie almost dropped the cooler from surprise when a hand reached from behind her and caught it. Sure her worst fears were confirmed, she whirled around only to find herself face-to-face with an older version of Jesse.

"Sorry, I didn't mean to startle you," Mark said. His slight smile told her he knew that for a brief second she'd thought it was Jesse behind her. He held out his hand in greeting. "I guess we've never formally been introduced. I'm Mark Daniels."

His smile was almost identical to his younger brother's. Mark's hair was grayer and his build wasn't quite as athletic as Jesse's, but the family resemblance was uncanny.

Not a little embarrassed, Rennie shook his hand and then stepped back. "I don't know how we've missed each other before this, but it's nice to finally meet you. I've heard a lot about you."

"I hope at least part of it was complimentary."

"Most of it," Rennie assured him. Before she could say anything else, Vickie walked up.

"Don't tell him any specifics, Rennie. It's hard enough to live with his ego." She looped her arm through Mark's, the expression on her face making it clear how she really felt about him.

"Where do you want this stuff, Vickie?"

"We've got tables set up out back on the deck. We decided to arrange everything as a buffet and let everyone find a seat wherever they can. Go set your basket down and grab something cold to drink." Vickie gave her husband a wicked smile. "Come on, champ, I've signed us up to play the winners of this volleyball game."

Rolling his eyes. Mark let his petite wife pull him toward the crowd of players waiting for the current round to end. Rennie did as Vickie suggested, calling out greetings to several other friends as she walked around to the deck.

She carried her basket and cooler to the cedar deck. After unloading the food, she looked around for a place to stow the basket until she'd need the utensils.

"If you're looking for the seats that Becky picked out for us, it's that table over there. The one with the big reserved sign on it."

This time Rennie knew her luck had indeed run out. Slowly she turned around. Jesse was coming out the back door, carrying a heaping tray of hamburgers and hot dogs. Wearing a bright red apron with KISS THE COOK emblazoned across the front, he obviously had volunteered to oversee the barbecue.

Rennie was at a loss for words. Her mind was going in too many directions at once for her thoughts to be coherent. Jesse's presence brought out such mixed reactions. Intellectually, she was sure she should just pick up her basket and go back home. Vickie would keep an eye on Becky, so she wouldn't be spoiling her daughter's day.

In her traitorous heart, though, she knew that secretly she'd been hoping he'd be there. It felt so good to see him, to spend time with him, even if she knew there was no hope for them.

Evidently her lack of response told Jesse more than her words could have.

"If it makes you uncomfortable to have me eat with you, I'll make some excuse to the girls. Honest, Rennie, I didn't want to trap you into something. Becky wanted to eat with Brittany, who wanted to eat with me. No pressure, I promise."

His smile was tentative. It hurt Rennie to see the usually self-confident Jesse feeling so unsure of his welcome. She hastened to put him at ease.

"Don't be silly, Jesse. Even if we can't be . . . uh, special friends"—Rennie caught herself just in time, barely avoiding saying that they might have been lovers—"we can still be . . . uh, friends," she finished lamely. She had to sound like an idiot to Jesse.

"Okay," he said, the spark in his eyes telling her that he knew what had flustered her. "We'll be friends, not *friends*."

"Oh, just shut up, Jesse Daniels! You know what I meant."

Rennie tried to stare him down but ended up laughing along with him. She'd almost forgotten that besides the strong sexual attraction she felt for the man, she honestly liked his company. It had been years since she'd known a man that she could relax and laugh with.

"Before the crowd gets too hungry, tell me how you'd like your burgers. I told the girls we'd have to eat early so that I'd be able to cook for everyone else. If I don't, Mark will take over, and I want him to have a chance to relax and enjoy himself. Hope that's okay."

"No problem. Make both of ours well done. Hold the mustard on hers; go heavy on the onions on mine."

"Lots of onions, huh? Guess you're not expecting a date to meet you here, then." He tried to sound flippant, but his brown eyes revealed his very real concern.

"There's no one else, Jesse. You know that," Rennie sighed. "How about you? Did you make your peace with Vanessa?"

"She's not that forgiving. Besides, I'm not interested." He changed the subject, much to Rennie's relief. "Have I ever told you how good I am at hamburgers?"

Rennie leaned against the side of the deck as Jesse began covering the grill with patties. "No, I have to admit that was one particular topic we never got around to discussing."

"Watch this." His hands just flew, turning one burger right after the other. He even flipped a couple up in the air, catching them just in the nick of time.

"Wow, I am impressed. Where did you develop this remarkable talent?"

"College. I went to school on the fast-food plan. Besides inspiring the art students on campus in all of my glory during the day, I cooked my way through for one of the hamburger joints near the college in the evening."

Rennie was finally relaxing, enjoying Jesse's good-natured banter. "Tell me, did you wear more clothing for your night job."

Jesse laughed, his smile special for her alone. "Of course. I had to protect my, um, assets. If I had damaged the goods, I'd have lost my modeling job." The burgers were rapidly getting done. "Can you run in and get me a platter? If I leave these on much longer, I'll ruin my reputation as a chef."

When she returned, Rennie asked, "Are we about ready to eat? If so, I'd better round up the girls."

Jesse nodded, concentrating on the barbecue. Rennie picked up her basket and set places for the girls, Jesse, and herself. The girls, who had been playing on the swing set, came running when they saw Rennie pouring drinks.

In short order, they were all gathered around the table, their plates overflowing with food. Whether it was by accident or deliberate on someone's part, Jesse ended up sitting next to Rennie. She was conscious of every move he made. His arm brushed hers when he reached for the potato chips. His leg touched hers when he leaned across the table to help Brittany open her drink.

By the time they finished eating, every nerve ending she had was tingling, aching for Jesse's touch. The intermittent contact had been at once too much and not enough. From the look on his face, Jesse was unaffected by what was going on. Rennie, on the other hand, wasn't sure how much more she could take without screaming out of sheer frustration.

Following him back to his station as chief cook, she gave herself a stern talking to. She was just enjoying a friend's company. Nothing more. If a small voice in her mind told her that Jesse was far more than just a friend, she did her best to ignore it.

The afternoon passed by in a hurry. When Mark insisted on taking over as cook for a while, Jesse just naturally kept Rennie at his side. And no matter what else he was doing, he let her know that he was glad she was there.

They played a hard-fought game of volleyball. When their side retired undefeated, Jesse led the way to where some of the adults were relaxing. He collapsed in the shade, pulling Rennie down beside him. With only a little coaxing, she let him rest his head in her lap. He closed his eyes and gave every appearance of drifting off to sleep.

Rennie took the opportunity to study his face in repose. Her hands ached to touch him, but she dared not. She already knew how addicting Jesse could be for her. For the moment, she contented herself to just memorize every feature of his face. A strange thing to do for a woman bent on keeping a man out of her life.

Just then, she happened to look up in time to catch Mark and Vickie exchange knowing looks as they walked by.

Oh, no, she thought. They were obviously jumping to the conclusion that she and Jesse were back to being an item. Nothing could be further from the truth. Right?

But if it wasn't true, what was she doing sitting here in front of everyone, acting like she was Jesse's date. They hadn't come together, but they'd been inseparable for hours. Even Becky was acting as if it was perfectly natural for her mother to be with Jesse.

What could she have been thinking of? For now, she couldn't do much but sit and wait for Jesse to wake up. Then she could make a discreet exit, maybe claiming a headache. With an ache somewhere in the vicinity of her heart, she took what pleasure she could from having Jesse close to her for the moment. Absolutely, positively, this was the last time she would let herself get caught up in the excitement of being with him.

Next time, well, there just wouldn't be a next time. Her traitorous heart couldn't be trusted to remain impervious to his charm.

Jesse stood in the front window, watching Rennie walking away from the house, actually almost running away. Not once did she look back. He smiled. His lady didn't know it, but she wasn't fooling anyone but herself if she thought that leaving the barbecue early was going to save her from one Jesse Daniels.

He knew to the moment when it had occurred to Rennie that she had again let her guard down with him. He'd been feigning sleep, knowing that was the only way that Rennie would feel safe with him.

Just the feel of her thighs beneath his head was enough to send a rush of heated desire coursing through him. He was just barely able to keep from acting on impulse. When his body's reaction to her nearness might have become too obvious to even a casual observer, he'd stirred in his "sleep" and turned over to hide the evidence.

Shortly afterward, she'd stiffened and jerked away the hand that had been resting on his shoulder. As tempting as it was to stay where he was, he relented and sat up, acting as if he'd just woken up.

After all, his plan was to make her comfortable in his presence and to remind her how much they enjoyed each other's company. If he made her too skittish, it would be that much harder to lull her into trusting him the next time.

And there definitely would be a next time. He'd see to it.

"One down, sixteen more to go," Rennie muttered under her breath as she helped stack the last of the club's sleeping bags out of the way.

"Did you say something, Mom?" Becky asked.

"What? Oh, no, honey. I was just counting sleeping bags."

Satisfied, Becky ran off to join her friends in line to wait for the start of the whale workshop.

"Sounded more like you were counting the number of hours left until this campout is over with," said a nearby fellow leader.

Rennie shrugged and smiled sheepishly. "You know I usually look forward to these annual sleep-overs at the Seattle Science Center, but this time I'll be really glad to get back home."

"Anything wrong?"

"No, not really. It's partially because I've not been sleeping well for some reason this week, and I'm more tired than usual. Mainly, though, we've had real problems getting it organized this time. The two parents I can usually count on to come had to back out. Then the clutch went out on my van. I wasn't sure until last night if I'd have it back in time to drive it down here. You know, the usual 'if it can go wrong, it will.' "

"Let me know if there's anything my group can help you with. They're a couple of years older than your club, and it would be good experience for them."

"Thanks, but right now everything seems under control." That is, if she could manage one night's sleep without being haunted by dreams of Jesse Daniels and his big brown eyes.

Rennie joined the girls and did a nose count. Then she did it again. They were short at least two girls and one adult.

"Girls, can you tell me who we're missing?"

They all looked around, and then Brittany spoke up. "Jennifer told me yesterday that she wasn't coming. The only other ones I can think of are Darcey and her mom."

Rennie was worried now. Trailblazer required the presence of at least two adults with each club at all times, and Mrs. Woods was the only parent who'd said she'd be able to come. If she didn't show soon, Rennie would have to start trying to track down another volunteer. She explained her problem to the leader of the neighboring group so she could keep an eye on the girls while Rennie did some checking.

"Girls, may I have your attention? While you're learning about whales and doing your art projects, I'll go find a phone and see where Mrs. Woods and Darcey are."

"What happens if they're not coming, Mrs. Sawyer?" Brittany asked. "Will we have to go home?"

"I'm sure they're just delayed in traffic. Don't worry," Rennie assured her, hoping she sounded more confident than she felt.

Fifteen minutes and several phone calls later, Rennie was getting desperate. She'd reached Mr. Woods on the first call, only to find out that Mrs. Woods was at the emergency room having Darcey's hand x-rayed. She'd shut it in the car door on their way to leave for the sleep-over.

Added to that, evidently most of the other parents had taken advantage of the girls being gone for the night to make plans to go out. Her last hope was Vickie, whose line was busy. Rennie waited another minute before dialing again.

"Hello," Vickie answered.

"Oh, Vic, thank goodness you're home!" Rennie exclaimed.

"Rennie? What's wrong? Is Brittany okay?"

"Yes, Brittany's okay. It's Mrs. Woods and Darcey. Mrs. Woods was supposed to be here tonight as the other adult with the club, but Darcey hurt her hand so they can't come. I've got to find another adult to fill in or I'll have to bring the girls back home. To top it all off, most of the other parents aren't even home."

"Sounds desperate," Vickie answered, sounding thoughtful.

"Do you think you could rescue me?" Rennie asked, crossing her fingers.

"Help will be on its way shortly," Vickie assured her.

"Oh, thank you, thank you, thank you." Rennie added, "I owe you a big one for this."

"Try to remember that."

"What?" Rennie asked, not understanding the tone of Vickie's statement.

"Nothing. Just remember that desperate times call for desperate measures. I'll have to make a couple of calls, but we'll save this somehow."

Relieved, Rennie went back to share the good news with the girls. The sleep-over was still on.

"Please be there, please," Vickie said into the receiver as she listened to the phone ringing on the other end of the line.

When Jesse's answering machine kicked on, she almost hung up without listening to the message. She was glad she didn't when she heard Jesse's recorded words.

"I'm not home right now, but I will be calling in for messages. Please leave your name and number and I'll get back to you as soon as I can. Thank you."

After the beep, Vickie spoke slowly and carefully. "Jesse, it's Vickie. I'm at home. If you want the opportunity of a lifetime to impress your lady, call me as soon as possible."

There was nothing Vickie could do then but hang up and wait. If Jesse didn't pick up his messages in the next half hour, she'd have to break the news to Mark that their hot date for the night was canceled because she'd have to go to the sleep-over herself.

On the other hand, it just might be worth making the trip anyway to see Rennie's face when she saw Jesse coming to her rescue.

"How soon's Mom going to be here?" Brittany asked.

Glancing at her watch, Rennie said, "Should be soon. I talked to her just over an hour ago. She had to make some phone calls before she could leave, so I'd say it might be another fifteen to twenty minutes."

The girls were sitting in the back row of a group about to start a sing-a-long. It was time last planned activity before they all broke up into their separate clubs and settled in for the night. If Vickie didn't show up soon, Rennie was afraid she'd have to start loading the girls into the van to head back home.

She was watching the door for Vickie's familiar petite figure, so she didn't recognize Jesse until he was just a few feet away. He stood in front of her, his dress jacket slung carelessly over his shoulder.

Brittany was the first to speak. "Uncle Jesse, what are you doing here?" She jumped up and threw her arms around him for a hug.

He looked over Brittany's head at Rennie as he answered his niece, "Would you believe someone called for a white knight to come rescue some fair damsels in distress?"

"Was this Vickie's idea or yours?" Rennie asked, her gray eyes narrow with suspicion.

"She called me to see if I could fill in. She and Mark had theater tickets they couldn't return and I wasn't doing anything important."

The girls moved over to make room for him to join them and Rennie on the floor. He gracefully folded his long legs and sank down beside Rennie as the singing started.

It was then she realized he was wearing a tuxedo. And looking great in it.

She leaned over and whispered, "Not doing anything important, huh? Do you always rent a tux for the evening just to sit around your condo? Poor man, all dressed up and nowhere to go."

"That's not the case at all. I own the tux." His brown eyes twinkled with good humor.

"That's not what I meant and you know it."

"Seriously, then. I was at a business dinner when I checked my phone messages. Vickie had left word on my answering machine that I should call her back as soon as possible. I called, she asked, I'm here. Any more questions?"

He was talking softly so close to her ear that Rennie could feel the warmth of his breath on her neck. She had trouble gathering her thoughts enough to speak at all.

"How long can you stay? Is Vickie coming after the theater lets out?"

"I'm here as long as you need me, which I assume is all night."

Did his voice sound a bit huskier when he mentioned spending the night with her, or was that her imagination at work? Hazy pictures of Jesse meeting her needs all night long flashed through her mind. Suddenly the Science Center was feeling uncomfortably hot.

"If you're sure, Jess. If you need to get back to the dinner, I can go try calling the other parents again."

Jesse turned to face her, his eyes holding hers prisoner.

"Rennie," he said patiently, "listen to me carefully. I'm here because you need me to be here. Nothing, I repeat, nothing is more important than that."

They were starting to get strange looks from others sitting near them, so Rennie stopped talking for the moment. She'd have more to say when the girls were settled in for the night.

When the color guard retired the flag, Rennie led her girls away from the gathering and back to the area that was reserved for them for the night. She was kept busy for the next half hour, finding lost packs, unsticking recalcitrant zippers, and making one last trip to the restroom.

Still, she was always aware of Jesse and what he was doing. He helped arrange sleeping bags. He showed Brittany a safe place to keep her glasses for the night. He laughed and joked with all the girls, for all the world looking like a man happy to be in the midst of eight-year-old girls and the chaos surrounding them.

Rennie started to spread out her own bag in the middle of the group but decided that she'd better sleep on the outer edge in case she needed to act as escort on any late-night bathroom runs. Besides, she couldn't very well leave Jesse sitting on the cold, hard floor. After a moment's thought, she asked Becky and Brittany to share her bag, which was larger than a normal sleeping bag. She spread Becky's bag out for herself and then offered Brittany's to Jesse.

"Do you think we'll actually be able to sleep?" he asked, arching an eyebrow in disbelief.

"Sure," she answered smugly. "On a good sleep-over, I usually manage to get in at least an hour or so."

"Oh, good. For a while there I was afraid I wouldn't get my normal quota of z's." He stood by his assigned sleeping spot and removed his black tie and rolled up his sleeves.

The sight of his strong forearms, tanned skin contrasting vividly with his white pleated shirt, had Rennie mesmerized. Then she watched in disbelief as Jesse wadded up his tuxedo jacket to use for a pillow. Before she could say anything, the overhead lights blinked on and off twice to warn everyone that it was almost time for lights-out.

"Is everyone settled?" she asked when she returned with the last group to use the restroom.

All the girls answered in the affirmative. Rennie looked around for her own bag, which wasn't where she'd put it.

Brittany and Becky had set it next to the one they were sharing, which was fine with Rennie. What bothered her, however, was the fact that it was also uncomfortably close to Jesse's. There was no way for her to move it now without disturbing the girls.

Besides, Jesse was watching her with just a hint of a smile. He had read her thoughts and was waiting to see how she'd react. Without a word, she gave a quick good-night kiss to Brittany and then Becky.

"Where's *my* kiss?" Jesse whispered softly so only Rennie could hear.

She pointedly ignored him as she crawled inside her sleeping bag, deliberately turning away from his disturbing presence. She thought she heard him whisper "Chicken!" but she couldn't be sure.

Amazingly, all the girls fell asleep with a minimum of giggling and talking. As silence descended, Rennie felt her own eyes growing heavy, her breathing rhythmic and slow. Her last conscious thought was that secretly she wished it was Jesse and herself that were sharing her sleeping bag built for two instead of Becky and Brittany.

Two hours later, the nightmare began. It started with Courtney waking Rennie to tell her that she felt sick to her stomach and her head hurt. Rennie touched the girl's forehead. She wasn't feverish, but her skin felt clammy.

"Honey, I'll have to get a hold of your folks to come get you. Lie down while I go call them." She tried to keep her voice low and calm, so they wouldn't wake up the others.

Jesse was sleeping so peacefully, Rennie hated to disturb him, but she couldn't leave the area without having someone to sit with Courtney. She tried shaking his shoulder, but he just batted her hand away with his. Then she tried calling his name. He frowned and snuggled deeper into the sleeping bag.

Any other time, she would have found his dedication to sleep as amusing as his aversion to mornings, but she had to have him alert and functioning. Finally, she jerked his tuxedo jacket out from under his head. That jarred him enough to force his eyes open.

"This better be good," he muttered as he sat up, rubbing his eyes.

"Sorry, sir, but I've got a sick kid who needs watching while I go call her folks."

"Which one?" he asked as he glanced around at the huddled forms.

"Courtney. She's over on that side of the group. I told her to lie down, but she may need to make a run for the bathroom. I'll be back as soon as I can."

By the time Rennie got back, two more girls had joined Courtney sitting up and holding their stomachs. Jesse was nowhere to be seen.

"Where's Mr. Daniels?" she asked the closest of the kids.

"He ran to the bathroom with Jenny. She was going to throw up on your sleeping bag."

"Oh, no," Rennie moaned. "Okay, I'll get another leader to sit with you while I go make some more calls. Tell Mr. Daniels that I'll be back as soon as I can."

This time, all the girls were awake and stirring around. Only four were sick so far, but there was too much commotion for the others to sleep.

It took longer this time for Rennie to get through to all of the parents. Under the circumstances, she'd have to send even the un-affected girls home. After talking to one mother, Rennie found out that the four sick ones had all attended the same birthday party before coming to the sleep-over. It appeared likely that the problem was food poisoning rather than the flu. Some parents were on their way to pick up their girls; the others would be waiting for Rennie to meet them at a local emergency room with the sick ones.

After the last call, Rennie came trudging back, feeling the cumu-lative effects of the last few days. Just as she reached the group, Jesse jumped up from the sleeping bag he'd been sitting on, grabbed up Courtney and ran for the restroom.

Rennie watched as his long legs ate up the distance, the sick girl cradled in his arms, his face determinedly smiling to reassure her. Rennie felt the warm stir of a powerful emotion in her heart and in her mind. Even if she refused to label it as anything stronger than admiration, there was no denying it was pulling her toward the man who'd just disappeared into the women's bathroom without even a hesitation in his step.

She'd been wrong about Jesse. He was more than a three-piece suit bent on success at any cost. She should have known that from the way his nieces felt about him. Even Becky, normally shy around men, had warmed to Jesse in ways that she'd never felt for her own father.

Rennie felt ashamed. Jesse had in fact committed some of the crimes as had Robin, but with one important difference—Jesse was willing to change. At the very least, she owed Jesse an apology for her lack of trust in him.

Just then, Rennie saw him come out of the bathroom. She groaned when she saw he was wearing only his undershirt with his dress slacks. She met him halfway and took Courtney from his arms.

"Please tell me that your lovely dress shirt isn't another casualty of this night," she asked after she made the girl comfortable on a nearby sleeping bag.

"First reports aren't very hopeful, but a good bleaching may revive the patient," he quipped.

"Jesse, I swear we've never had a sleep-over turn out like this. Do you hate me much for getting you in so deep?"

Perhaps he heard something in her voice or saw a different spark in her eyes, because he gave her a heart-stopping smile and pulled her into his arms for a hug. He held her close for a minute, letting her absorb some of his strength.

"Lady," he said for her ears alone, "haven't you figured out yet that I couldn't hate anything about you?"

The dawn of the new day was clear, the sky sprinkled with clouds painted in shades of fiery red and orange. If someone had told Rennie just hours ago that she'd greet the morning with a smile, she'd have laughed at the thought. Or maybe screamed.

Still, despite the grimness of the night, she was standing on her back deck with a cup of hot coffee in her hand, counting her blessings.

First, the night was over. Second, Becky wasn't among those

who'd gotten sick and ended up at the emergency room. In fact, right now she was at Vickie's house sharing Brittany's bunk bed.

But the most exciting aspect of the day was the fact that Jesse was here, in her house, in her shower. Rennie had thought about sneaking in and joining him under the steamy spray. However, until they'd talked about some of their misconceptions about each other, it was probably unwise to complicate their relationship any further.

Still, the idea was so very tempting.

Vickie had offered to keep Becky for the day ostensibly to let Rennie get some rest. In reality, Rennie suspected she was continuing in her role of self-appointed matchmaker. If time alone was what they needed, time alone is what they'd get.

Just as Rennie stepped back inside, she heard the shower shut off. She headed for the kitchen to pour Jesse another cup of coffee, then returned to the deck to wait.

In just a few minutes, she heard the sliding glass door open. Her nerve endings tingled with awareness at his approach. He slid his arms around her from behind and rested his head against hers. The shower had left his hair damp. It felt cool against her face, contrasting vividly with the warmth of his body pressed close to hers.

"We need to talk, you know," he murmured from somewhere close to her ear.

"I know."

Another moment of silence followed.

"I guess I should start, since I'm the one who so badly misjudged you." She turned in his arms to face him. "I'm so sorry I was punishing you for having a wardrobe like Robin's. I know now that the only resemblance was a superficial one."

"What about my car? Don't forget it made me an automatic winner in the yuppie game," he teased. Then he became serious. "Actually, other than clothes, it's the first major item I bought for myself that wasn't secondhand. I just finished paying off my student loans last year."

"Oh, no, now I feel even worse." Rennie buried her face against his chest.

"Honey, listen to me," Jesse said as he gently lifted her chin to face him. "I didn't tell you that to make you feel bad. I told you that because I wanted you to understand that you were partially right. The surface image was important to me because I could look in the mirror and tell myself that Mom was wrong; I could amount to something more than the worthless troublemaker she said I was."

A catch in his voice told Rennie that he still suffered from vestiges of the pain his mother had caused.

After a second, he took a deep breath and continued. "Still, underneath it all, I felt like that failure, and it almost cost me you. If you saw through the facade that easily, then maybe she was right all along. If Vickie hadn't knocked some sense into me, I'd have never had the courage to come after you."

By then Rennie had tears running down both cheeks. Jesse gently kissed them away, then settled his mouth over hers. It was a kiss of healing and promise.

"I know I'm not dressed for any formal declarations of undying passion," Jesse said, glancing down at the faded sweats he'd borrowed from Mark that morning. "But, Rennie, do you have any idea how much I love you?"

"If it's anything like how much I love you, it's a pretty staggering amount," she answered shyly.

His grin competed with the sun for brightness. "In that case, do you think we should get back at Vickie for her matchmaking by letting her plan a wedding as fast as she can arrange it? Maybe we'll even force her to make bridesmaid dresses for Becky, Brittany, and Lexi."

"A wedding?" Rennie asked, her lungs struggling to breathe.

"You will, won't you? I mean, will you do me the honor of marrying me?" For a brief moment all his self-doubt shone in his gentle brown eyes.

"Oh, yes, Jesse, yes!"

They kissed to seal their promise just as the sun cleared the horizon in a final burst of color. Together, they would face the new day, a new beginning.

Epilogue

"Now, remember. I'm just the muscle this year," Jesse said as he opened the twin garage doors.

"Yes, dear."

"I mean it. No paperwork, no late-night runs for more candy. No nothing."

"Yes, dear." A giggle escaped, causing Jesse to frown. "I promise, really I do.

"Okay, now stand back and let a man do his work."

Jesse watched as a large truck pulled up in front of the house and parked. It was the same one that had changed his life the year before. He waited to see if the same driver climbed down out of the cab.

Yep, it was him all right. He even had the same forklift on the trailer behind the truck. And, of course, the merchandise he was unloading looked depressingly familiar.

"You understand that your delicate condition is the only reason that I'm here at all."

Rennie laughed. "Face it, Counselor, I look about as delicate as that truck out there. I'm not due for four weeks. I can handle the candy sale," she assured him.

Jesse looked at his very pregnant wife and gave her a special smile. To him, she was everything that was beautiful and precious in the world.

Very firmly, he repeated, "I'm the muscle. I don't want to see you lifting even as much as a single box of that stuff." Shaking his head, he said, "I can't believe that for the second year in a row, I'm having to park my new car outside to make room for chocolate."

"Yeah, but the station wagon can take it," Rennie told him. "Besides, this is not my fault. When I offered to take over as candy mom for Vickie because she'd have a new baby to contend with, how was I to know that her condition was catching?"

Jesse happened to glance over just as she rubbed the side of her stomach.

"Junior acting up again?" he asked, pleasure mixed with concern. He placed his hand over hers, both of them caught up in the wonder of the miracle that they had created together.

"You go in and rest for now. I can handle this part." He gave her a quick kiss and pushed her toward the kitchen door.

Thirty minutes later, the garage was filled with the usual assortment of Trailblazer candy. Jesse decided that he might as well take time to sort it out for the individual clubs. That way there'd be no reason for Rennie to do more than he thought was good for her.

"Honey," he called, "can you bring me the club order sheets?" He heard her approach. Jesse decided to tease her a bit as he made room near the door for a larger-than-average number of boxes.

After the last sale, Mrs. Billings had been given a special reward for selling enough candy to send four needy girls in her club to summer camp for a week. Rumor had it she was going to try to break her own record this year. Jesse had to admire her dedication, but that didn't stop him from groaning dramatically as he added yet another case to her pile of candy.

Without looking at Rennie, he said, "Part of the bargain, you'll remember, is that I don't have to be here when Mrs. Billings picks up her share of this stuff tomorrow night. My back won't take the strain."

From the doorway, Rennie said, "I'm sorry, but I may not be able to keep that particular promise."

"Oh, no, you don't!" he started to protest. Then he saw the dazed expression on his wife's face. He leaped over a stack of peanut brittle to get to her. "What's wrong?" he demanded.

"Evidently Junior's decided that you have to handle the sale after all." She sat down abruptly on a handy stack of candy.

Jesse was speechless. For a moment, neither his voice nor his legs would work. He managed to sputter. "He, it, you . . ."

"Yes, exactly," Rennie said, smiling up at him. "My water broke. The doctor will meet us in the emergency room." When Jesse didn't move, she tried again. "He prefers not to make house calls, Jess.

Don't you think we'd better get my suitcase and start on our way to the hospital?"

That stirred Jesse into action. He scooped Rennie up in his arms and, despite her protests that she could walk, carried her out to their new family car.

When he had her settled in and her seat belt fastened, Jesse ran back into the house. He returned in record time, suitcase in hand. When he climbed into the driver's side, he told Rennie, "I called Vickie. She'll keep Becky for us and bring her down to the hospital later." With that, they were on their way.

"Only for you and your mom, kid," Jesse murmured softly to the baby resting in his arms.

Sleepily Rennie asked, "What's that?"

Jesse could hardly look away from his son's face. "I was just explaining to our son that only for the two of you would I again face the horrors of candy commandos."

Rennie just smiled. She knew her husband loved her and would always share the burdens of parenthood with her. In the year that they'd been married, Jesse had already done more with Becky than Robin had in six times that long.

"You know, if you think about it, we really do owe a lot to the candy sale." Her eyes were bright with amusement despite her obvious fatigue. It had been a long night for both of them.

Jesse met his wife's gaze and shook his head. "Who'd have thought that I'd owe all my happiness to nut clusters and peanut brittle?" He crossed the room and gently snuggled the baby into Rennie's waiting arms.

Watching the play of emotions across her face as Rennie nursed their son, Jesse felt a warmth of happiness settle in his heart. It was another reminder that the problem of her world versus his world no longer existed.

Side by side, they'd built their own world filled with love, and laughter, and a future they'd share together.